The Bill

The Bill 4

JOHN BURKE

Thames Mandarin

A Thames Mandarin Paperback

THE BILL 4

First published in Great Britain 1990
by Mandarin Paperbacks
Michelin House, 81 Fulham Road, London SW3 6RB
in association with
Thames Television International Ltd
149 Tottenham Court Road, London W1P 9LL

Mandarin is an imprint of the Octopus Publishing Group

Novel copyright © 1990 John Burke
Television Scripts © 1989 Geoff McQueen,
Christopher Russell, Al Hunter, Barry Appleton and J. C. Wilshire

A CIP catalogue record for this book
is available from the British Library
ISBN 0 7493 0374 3

Printed and bound in Great Britain
by Cox & Wyman Ltd, Reading

One

There were two of them within a few hundred yards of each other. In both cases the smell was something the most optimistic con-man would hardly have considered bottling and trying to flog as an aphrodisiac, or even as a public toilet air freshener. The smoke of a couple of fires vigorously burning rubbish did little to improve the stench hanging over the building site or the quayside.

The money being poured into dockside development had not yet begun to pay any healthy dividends in this squalid sector. The first boom of apartment-block building had become less of a big bang than a spasmodic splutter. The gutted shells of old warehouses had not been replaced by the promised desirable residences for City commuters; and the Docklands railway seemed to have been planned to avoid any detour around this spur of Thamesside land.

Picking his way behind the foreman across an obstacle course of dockland development, PC Malcolm Haynes was not sure whether to hold his nose to avoid asphyxiation or keep both hands free for the moment when he tripped over something unmentionable and fell into the middle of something equally unmentionable. Not far away, hidden by the debris of buildings coming slowly down and the skeletal framework of buildings going slowly up – with the demolished ones looking rather more stylish than the new ones – PC George Garfield found his stomach having much the same trouble with the stench from the river mud.

Scrabbling for a foothold on a mound of waste, Haynes demanded: 'Mr Bell, just where is she?'

'She's dead,' said Tyrone Bell. 'That's all there is to it. Definitely dead.'

'We still have to see her.'

'I know that. Wouldn't have sent for you otherwise, now would I?'

'We have to get a doctor to certify it as well.'

The foreman plodded over a mound of slime-green wood as if this was an unremarkable part of his health-giving daily stroll. He was a man as stained and dusty as his surroundings, with pale lips and crooked teeth. Every few minutes he wiped his hands on his overalls, just as likely to acquire more grime on his fingers as to shift it on to his clothes. 'Don't need to tell me. We seem to spend half our time nowadays ringing you lot about 'em.'

An unidentifiable bird swooped down onto a heap of unidentifiable rags and splinters, and veered away under Haynes' nose. Whatever genus of bird it was, the wind of its passing left lingering evidence of its unsavoury appetites.

Haynes made an effort to sound crisp and authoritative. 'Just how many bodies have you had, then?'

'Lost count. Dead tramps, most of them. Turn up on all the sites round here. The cold gets 'em.' Bell stopped at last beside an inverted rubbish skip. A grimy arm stuck out from beneath one side of the half painted, half rusted metal. 'Here we are, then.'

Haynes stooped and tried to take the woman's pulse. He regretted it. Whether she had always smelt like that or was beginning to do so after her spell under the skip, he could not tell. Nor did he want to take too close a look into the shadowy sockets of her eyes, dead yet somehow furtively greedy, peering out through a gap in the soggy newspapers and boxes she had packed in between the ground and the edge of the skip. Detailed examination was for forensic. Haynes would be only too glad to hand over responsibility to them.

'Right, then. Don't touch her.'

'Wouldn't fancy it,' Bell assured him.

'I'll radio in and get somebody to take her off your hands.'

6

'Wouldn't let my hands near her,' said Bell even more fervently.

At the same time George Garfield had been reluctantly following a gruff old age pensioner along the bank of the King William Docks to Minister Wharf, getting more and more doubtful about the whole set-up. The old dodderer had sounded earnest enough when he had stopped the PC on the road to the wharf, but now his wheezings and mutterings began to sound like those of some senile eccentric who had lost his way, mentally as well as physically.

'Look, Mr Jeffries, are you quite sure . . .?'

'Along here a bit.' The old man was puffing more and more alarmingly. He stumbled, and tried to focus rheumy eyes on the cluttered ground ahead. 'I come here earlier on, right?' The effort of stooping and picking up a couple of jam jars filled with yellowish water brought on a fit of coughing. When he had brought it under control he gasped: 'Fishing this morning, see. Didn't notice anything at first, then it began to get me. I'm . . . I'm a bit asthmatic. Thought I could smell something getting on my chest. And you know what I reckon it was?'

'Come on, is this a wind-up? I got things to do.'

'Straight up, I'll show you. I know where it's coming from an' all.'

Jeffries dug into a ragged waistcoat pocket and produced an inhaler. Two sniffs, and he let out a moan. It was finished. For a moment he snuffled desperately at it, then thrust it towards Garfield as if holding him personally responsible. He tried to croak out something; but his knees sagged, and in unnerving slow motion he crumpled to the ground.

Garfield swore. Going down on his knees on the muddy edge of the wharf, he began a rhythmic heart massage. There was no response. Desperately he tried mouth-to-mouth; but every breath of riverside fumes he inhaled was so foul that he wondered if he wasn't putting paid to the old man by passing it on. To make it worse, his own head was beginning to swim.

7

He sat up, groping for his radio. Even within his own head he could hear how faint and weirdly irregular his voice was.

'Urgent assistance. 572 to any unit. Urgent assistance, Minister Wharf. Need an ambulance . . . man in distress. And . . . not feeling too good myself.'

From the CAD room WPC June Ackland's voice broke in demanding a response from anyone in the vicinity of Minister Wharf. Haynes replied at once, snapping out a quick report on the corpse already discovered, before moving off to see if there was a way of saving someone else from becoming a corpse.

From a ridge of rubble above the wharf he got a whiff of something even more lethal than the air Tyrone Bell had introduced him to. The muddy bank seemed to be breathing out a poison all of its own. Caught in it were the huddled shapes of an elderly man and, rocking on hunched knees over him like a lover slowly caressing the breast and kissing the lips of an unresisting lover, PC George Garfield. Haynes leaped over a heap of sand and slowed himself to avoid plunging off the quay into the greasy, slowly heaving water below. It was only as he groped down the last of the slippery steps to the two men that he realised the urgency of Garfield's message. His right hand had fallen away limply; he was struggling for breath, no longer able to offer it to the sprawled victim on the ground.

'What the hell . . .?'

Garfield turned his head and tried to grin a welcome. His usually chubby, boyishly enthusiastic face was growing wan and sickly by the second. 'Fumes,' he whispered. 'Got to move him out.'

Haynes leaned over the motionless old man and took his turn at mouth-to-mouth resuscitation. Beside him, in a slow echo of his own pumping of breath, he heard Garfield wheeze: 'Too near, Malc. Don't . . . not you as well. Got to get out of this.'

The smell was overpowering. Haynes tried not to notice, tried to force life back into the man sprawled in the mud; and,

8

just as he began to get the feeblest of responses, realised that Garfield had passed out completely.

The swish and scrape of tyres along the dockside was the loveliest sound he had heard in a long time. As they lifted Garfield and the old man away from the dizzying smell, he tried to give them a hand – only to find that they were supporting him too, and telling him to take it easy and stop reeling about all over the place.

'And would you believe, this very morning there's been a pompous old cow from the waste Regulation Authority round at Sun Hill, complaining about the police taking no action against fly-tippers polluting the dockside area?'

Haynes felt queasily that another couple of minutes above that mud and he would have been contributing to the dock-side pollution; and was not even sure he was going to make it safely back to the station.

He made it. Still pale and shaky, he listened muzzily to June Ackland and managed to add a mumbled confirmation of her report to Detective Constable Lines.

'An old lady vagrant,' said Ackland, 'snuffing it down on the docks. Foreman on the building site reckoned it was the cold.'

'So what's new? Even you woodentops don't need CID to figure that one out.'

'But five minutes later we get George Garfield and an OAP keeling over from fumes a couple of hundred yards away. And when Malcolm here leaves the old tramp and goes to render assistance, he nearly joins them in dreamland. I mean, *look* at him.'

Tosh Lines heaved his not inconsiderable weight around the end of the desk and took a good look at Haynes. The prospect did not seem to fill him with any enthusiasm.

'Hold it. You reckon this could be a bit of illegal chemical tipping?'

'Any better ideas?'

'Garfield's old man – '

'Still the worse for wear. No report yet.'

9

'And your old tramp?' Lines peered into Haynes' ashen face.

'Like June says, the site foreman reckons he gets plenty of them hiding away and dying of the cold before anybody even knows they're there.'

'Foreman?'

'Name of Bell. Mr Tyrone Bell.'

'Tyrone Bell,' breathed Lines. 'Site foreman now? Some building site that must be . . . run by a bloke I nicked for fly-tipping only a couple of months ago.' He thumped the edge of June's console. 'Nobody'll employ him as a driver any more, so he finds some mug to set him up looking after a nice big patch of building land. And what do you bet he's using it as cover for dumping chemicals?'

'And poisoning people,' said Haynes wretchedly.

June Ackland looked from one man to the other. 'So where do you start?'

'A few samples of the water would be a help.'

As if in answer to a magical summons Inspector Christine Frazer walked across the CAD room. Her uniform, like her sleek blonde hair, was as smart and unrumpled as ever. Yet she was not walking as trimly as usual: it would have been difficult for her to march in her normal aggressive way when holding out fastidiously before her a jam jar full of some viscous liquid. Detective Inspector Burnside, following her in, might have enjoyed the spectacle if only he could have been sure what it was all about.

Frazer offered the jar to the detective constable.

'A sample, DC Lines? I ordered it myself. What do you think we should do with it?'

Whatever other temptations might have crossed his mind, Burnside managed to say levelly: 'Could make Bob Cryer a cup of tea with it.'

Frazer gave him a cool, steady glance. 'I've got a better idea. As this is likely to be a case of illegal waste disposal, we ought to send the sample along to the appropriate council body. Get

10

that friend of yours at the Waste Regulation Authority to push it through their laboratory and analyse it.'

Burnside smiled a smile of genuine admiration. 'The way that busybody was going on at us . . . yes, why not? She bungs complaints and extra work our way. Let's bung some of it hers.' He turned back, put his head out of the door, and bellowed up the stair-well. 'Dashwood! Come here. I've got an errand for you.'

Early that afternoon Haynes, still much the worse for wear, began the drudgery of picking up threads and seeing if the resources of Sun Hill could weave them into some coherent pattern.

He began with a fruitless call on the station collator's files, but for once the resourceful Cathy Marshall had nothing to offer. There were not enough personal details yet on the corpse, and no particular reason to suppose the old woman had had a criminal record. Cathy suggested a visit to the local Salvation Army hostel; and it was on their recommendation that Haynes finished up at an unsavoury building standing like an insecure survivor of bomb damage on the edge of a dusty main road. A condemned house with a wide gash all the way down one wall, overdue for demolition, it was in temporary use outside for a display of graffiti none too flattering to the police or the current housing authorities, and inside as a home for a motley collection of squatters. The one who answered the door was a youngish woman who already looked not only old but vengefully anxious to take out her miseries on whoever came carelessly within range. Three sullen-faced children fidgeted behind her. Someone had already taught them to leer contemptuously at policemen, and the graffiti outside would have helped that education along.

'Well?'

Afternoon, officer, said Haynes wryly and silently to himself. Aloud he said: 'Afternoon, madam. I'm making some inquiries – '

'You've got five seconds before I slam this door in your face.'

'What do you think I am, a door-to-door salesman?' Haynes' temper was as sour as the aftertaste of that building site and quayside. He was in no mood for this sort of thing. Then, before she could really fulfil her threat of closing the door, he snapped: 'Do you know an old lady called Gertie?'

'No. Why?'

'A man at the Sally Army place said her name was Gertie, and she used to sleep here sometimes. An old lady, always dressed in red. Very dirty face.'

'And the rest of her. What d'you wanna know for?'

'She died last night. I'm trying to trace any relatives.'

'She didn't have none.'

'But she did live here?'

'She didn't live here. She slept here if she got in without us noticing.'

'Sounds like you didn't get on.'

The woman's thin mouth twisted. 'Look. Just 'cos we have to get by in a place like this, don't mean we have to put up with nutters. She refused to wash, right. Did you ask them why they wouldn't have her at the shelter? Did you, eh? Flaming nuisance she was. If you ask me, she's better off dead.'

'I'll not bother putting you down for the funeral, then?'

'Get lost.' This time the squatter did slam the door.

The trouble was, she was probably right about poor old Gertie. Better off dead. Haynes glanced up at the house and made a quick appraisal of the surrounding area. Living here couldn't be all that far from being dead. His gaze ended up with relief on his watch. It was time to go back to Sun Hill.

As he crossed the road, a Sierra swung in beside the kerb.

DI Burnside's blue-shadowed chin jutted out of the open window. Beside him, DC Lines was already reaching back to open a rear door, while Burnside grinned that heavily emphatic, derisive grin of his. 'Weren't thinking of knocking off, were you, Malc?'

'Well, yes.'

'Well, no. Not yet you're not, mate. Your Gertie lady looks like she could turn into a biggie.' Burnside jerked his head towards the back seat. 'Care to accompany us, as we say?'

Tosh Lines' driving was as abrupt and aggressive as his boss's manner of interrogating a suspect. Maybe Tosh guessed that Burnside wanted to be hyped up for just that. The moment the car had stopped in a small whirlwind of grit on the building site he was out and on his way towards Tyrone Bell, standing in the doorway of a portacabin. The recently appointed foreman did not look happy at this unexpected visitation. He looked less happy when Haynes led the way to the skip where the old woman's body had been found.

Burnside studied the scene for a moment, then bent and sniffed at the edge of the skip. He wrinkled his nose. 'I'm not a happy man, Mr Bell.'

'Why's that, then?' The foreman wiped his hands on the sides of his overalls, trying to look sincerely puzzled and innocent and helpful all at the same time.

'We think you've been lying. Or anyway not going into too many details about the truth. And I'm going to prove it. Tosh, give Mike a shout. He's at the town hall with that Dr Reece. Tell him to get her down here pronto.'

'Right, guv.' Lines moved over to the car radio while Burnside turned his attention dourly back to Bell.

'There's a nasty smell round here. And not just what's coming up out of that ground or out of the river. You and I are going back to your office, Tyrone, and we'll wait there until I've had this site turned over. And if my friend from the Waste Authority doesn't find anything untoward I might let you go home.'

Dr Jane Reece from the Authority did not look the least bit like a friend of Burnside's when she arrived in DC Mike Dashwood's car. A forceful woman in her mid-thirties, with taut lips and eyes sharp enough to gouge the facts out of the muddiest heap of contamination, she could manage with the briefest gesture and the minimum number of words to make

13

it clear that she was an unrivalled expert in her own subject, that all who disagreed with her were ignorant and probably anti-social, and that policemen existed as servants of the public in general and herself in particular, and should not waste time on lesser matters while she was around. She established her attitude immediately she had stepped from the car.

'I fail to see why I had to be rushed here, inspector. Thanks to the sample already supplied by your station' – she allowed a condescending note of formal acknowledgment into her voice – 'we have already established with the fire brigade the likelihood of cleansing agents being dumped down a manhole next to this site. What do you expect me to add?'

'I don't know, doctor. But we'd rather it was more than a likelihood. And we want to know how it ties in with the other stuff that nearly laid out two of our uniformed branch.' Burnside chose the least hazardous path through the chaos towards the manhole and indicated that Haynes should remove the cover. 'I'd be the first one down there,' he said with unusual silkiness, 'if I thought it would do any good. Unfortunately only an expert like yourself can tell.'

Their glances crossed so sharply that Haynes half expected to be sprayed by a shower of sparks. Lifting the manhole cover to one side, he got an all too familiar waft of that awful smell – though nothing like as overpowering as that mixture of creeping fumes down by the water's edge.

Dr Reece permitted herself a wintry smile. 'It's as well I brought the appropriate clothing, isn't it?' She turned peremptorily to Mike Dashwood. 'Young man, will you fetch my overalls from your vehicle?'

Wriggling into overalls, she dug into a pocket for a plastic envelope of starch iodine paper, and edged herself down into the sewer shaft, her feet reaching for the iron rungs. Burnside smirked at Dashwood, but with a touch of admiration for the woman's unflappability.

When she emerged, she held out a shred of paper which

14

had turned blue. 'Undoubtedly an acidic cleansing agent. Illegal and very strong. And it looks like a very recent deposit.'

Burnside beamed. 'I'll go and break the news to our Mr Bell, and see what he's got to say.'

'I don't think you understand, inspector.'

'Sorry?'

'The cleansing agent is only half the story,' said Dr Reece crisply. 'It's bad, but not bad enough to kill. Which means the agent down there must have been mixed with some other chemical, somewhere between this point and the water, to create a toxic gas. Now, if I can find where that chemical comes into it, you might have a case. Especially if it has been dumped into the same system. I'd like to make a thorough search of the whole site.'

'Be my guest.' Burnside nodded Haynes and Tosh Lines to one side. 'Don't suppose we know what your lady tramp died of yet, do we?'

'Post-mortem won't be through until tomorrow morning at the earliest,' said Haynes.

'Mm. But I'm right in thinking that the old man at the docks got a skinful of these fumes, eh?'

'Oh, yes,' said Haynes grimly. 'Very bad.'

'How bad? Think he might be on his way out?'

'I'd be surprised if he makes it.'

'Near enough dead, then.' Burnside looked thoughtfully at Lines. 'Wonder how our precious Mr Bell will wear that bit of news?'

'It's not confirmed yet, guv. Nothing definite.'

'So far as Mr Bell is to know,' said Burnside, 'it's definite. That's how I'm going to spell it out for him.'

Understanding dawned on the DC. He nodded appreciatively. PC Haynes looked doubtful; then decided to nod as well. The three of them looked towards the distant figure of Tyrone Bell framed in his cabin doorway, watching them and wondering. Let him stew for a while; just a very little while.

Two

WPC Cathy Marshall's work as collator was generally acknowledged as superior to that of her predecessor, the whingeing Reg Hollis. For one thing, she was capable of smiling at things other than colleagues' disasters; and for another, she was efficient, and wanted to supply answers as quickly as both CID and the uniformed branch wanted them. Before coming on to Sun Hill strength in its Local Intelligence Office she had single-handedly dealt with a spectacular armed robbery, untangled the complexities of a widespread local fraud, and detected the first symptoms of villainy among a cartel of market traders. From all this she had learned the hard way what a hard-pressed officer wanted in an emergency and how fast it ought to be provided. Fighting off the advances of some Sun Hill men who had noticed that her shape, too, was different from Hollis's, she could have made a joke about what some of them wanted but were not going to get.

Cathy had two smiles, in fact: both spontaneous, but because of that very naturalness she was herself quite unaware of their effect. One was an instinctively friendly smile when she liked someone, accompanied by a glow in her dark brown eyes. If you found yourself on what was known as 'Cathy's coffee list', you could count yourself among the privileged few. The other smile, which almost invariably barred you from that list, was a sardonic little sidelong twitch of the lips suggesting she knew more about you than you would have wished.

Which she usually did. Small-time crooks and big-time villains were indexed and cross-referenced in vast detail in her files. She rarely needed to search through those files for long. Experience and a memory as good as any computer cataloguing system led her to the right place, the right character (or the character who by nature had always been wrong), and the right set of circumstances. But along with the professional or part-time criminals she had in her head another catalogue, to which she allowed no official access: those reflective eyes caught the characteristics of every officer in the station, fitted them into the right slot, and every now and then added to the store of information. In her rare idle moments she liked to sum up the present characteristics and future potential of the men and women around her, and sometimes regretted that the confidential nature of the job debarred her from laying bets on their ultimate destinies.

For instance, there was PC Richard Turnham. His lofty tone of voice and the occasional lift of his patrician eyebrows could irritate other men on the beat, even though they admitted that just by voice alone he came in useful for over-aweing awkward members of the public. The fact that he was a Cambridge graduate and had read Archaeology, Anthropology and Modern History, and also that his father was a senior civil servant capable of pulling a fair number of strings, was known to Chief Superintendent Brownlow, who was suitably courteous to such a talented officer and not above dropping hints about assignment to special duties and possible promotion at a remarkably early stage. This background was known also to Cathy, as well as his addiction to hockey and real tennis, sporting activities from which he blandly emerged with never a scar or bruise. One thing she could predict: he would not be plodding a routine beat for very long.

There were plenty of contrasts in Sun Hill. Nobody could have been less like Turnham than Detective Constable Alfred Lines. Tosh was as streetwise as any of the criminals he dealt with week in, week out: a roughneck with a true copper's nose for the job. Unlike the suave Turnham, he could expect little further promotion, and unlike Turnham he showed no signs of seeking it. He would have been no good at handling the increased responsibility or the internal politics. Always skint, he would have been glad of the extra money; but not at that price.

Still Cathy smiled, sympathising with people and enjoying their foibles rather than sneering. It made a great change indeed from the fussily collating, always unco-operative and often disruptive Hollis.

Right now she had dug out all the details of Tyrone Bell's previous misdemeanours for when Burnside needed them, and was engaged in assembling details of the career of the man Detective Sergeant Alastair Greig would be bringing in within the next few minutes. Bell was a clumsy second-rater, a blundering little petty crook rather than a top-flight villain. Whatever he had been up to this time, it ought not to take long to break him down. Eric Anthony Taylor was much bigger game; or had been in the not too distant past. Taylor had been a thorn in Burnside's none too sensitive flesh during several acrimonious encounters. He had worked with the top people and never been let down by any of them. The police knew the truth, but could never prove it. Under the hardest pressure nobody ever coughed on Taylor, and Taylor coughed on nobody. He always kept his cool, never lifting a hand against a policeman and never admitting to lifting a hand against anyone else, although a number of damaged skulls and broken limbs – other people's skulls and limbs – had marked the progress of his activities.

Doors swung to and fro along the corridor, their draught whistling faintly across the room as Greig and his prisoner marched into the custody area. Cathy poked her head round the corner to take a quick glance at the two men, with PC Able standing by. Tim Able was a keen young pavement pounder whose main ambition was to work his way on to the cars. He had a long way to go yet, though he was forever forcing the pace. His face now was keen and attentive, anxious for everyone to see that he was well and truly on the ball.

DS Greig's face was stony and unyielding. It was the lethal face of a hunter moving in for the kill. There was frequently

18

something unnerving about Alastair Greig, with his thinly incisive Aberdeen accent and eyes soured by the years he had spent with West End Central Vice Squad before coming to Sun Hill. Yet he had not severed his connection with the Metropolitan Police Band, and once when he had sat chatting cooly with Cathy he had suddenly warmed to the subject of Mozart and then of his collection of Johnny Dodds records. She had never heard him play the clarinet, but felt it might be a quite revealing experience. Though Greig was, on the whole, not the kind who would allow himself to reveal too much.

One glimpse of him at this moment was enough to tell her that he was in his most implacable and least musical mood. Taylor was not going to have an easy time of it. But then, Taylor himself looked just as stolid and impregnable. He had been given more than one rough ride by Burnside on previous occasions, and had never been thrown. With Burnside still coping with the toxic fumes business, it would be interesting to see how much more successful his subordinate could manage to be. Either way, prospects were not too good for Greig: if he let Taylor wriggle through his fingers, Burnside would roast him; if he succeeded where Burnside had failed, the result could be just as scorching.

Greig himself could hardly be unaware of the danger surrounding him. He remained almost too icily self-controlled as Sergeant Penny settled himself behind the charge room desk and asked formally: 'Has the prisoner been cautioned?'

'He has.'

Penny looked up at Taylor. 'You know why you've been arrested?'

'Some Mickey Mouse job I know nothing about.'

'At 8.30 p.m. on Friday the fifteenth of this month,' Greig intoned, 'an armed robbery took place at Melpax cash-and-carry in Pelling Way. The gang involved assaulted the manager and stole cash and tobacco products to a total value of £30,000. We have reason to believe this person was a member of that gang, and he is going to be questioned accordingly.'

It was suitably dry, routine and undramatic. The facts

19

behind it were far from routine or undramatic, certainly so far as the victims were concerned. Mr Arnold Redfern, the middle-aged manager of the small cash-and-carry, had seen from his office at the far end that four men were coming in through the main door, and took them for late customers. He soon discovered his mistake. The four were masked, and as he emerged unhurriedly from the office to join his girl assistant at the cash desk they were suddenly pushing him back against one of the shelves, out of sight of the window onto the street: two with handguns, one with a shotgun, one with a knife. Redfern had been slow to co-operate, not from bravery but because of the dizzying suddenness of the invasion. One of the men hit him; another turned to threaten the girl. It was easier that way. Joanne Kelly, trying to squeeze out of the narrow space between the cash desk and the wall, was grabbed and shaken to and fro until, scared witless, she blurted out where everything was – the safe, the storeroom door, the lot. The men emptied the till and began to clear the shelves. It was unfortunate that a passing police car should start off its siren. It was on its way to an accident, nothing to do with the raid; but the robbers were not to know that. Somebody panicked. Somebody threw Redfern to the floor and began kicking him; and on their way out one of them took a vicious swipe at him with the shotgun.

Outside, the man with the shotgun had slithered across a patch of oil and gone down for a moment. He was up again, piling into the van as it scraped against the edge of the door and rocketed away down the street. It was five minutes before the shivering Joanne Kelly could summon up the strength to lift the phone and quaver out her message.

All of which had led to Eric Taylor's arrival in the custody area at Sun Hill.

Penny sat with pen in hand, waiting. 'Could you tell me your full name and address, please?' When Taylor remained mute, folding his arms and gazing blankly at the wall, Penny unperturbedly began to write. 'The prisoner,' he murmured

20

aloud, 'refuses to give his name but is known to be Eric Anthony Taylor.'

Mike Dashwood collected the sheaf of papers Cathy Marshall had prepared, and made his way to the canteen. At a table in the corner, Alastair Greig had piled up an even more impressive folder of documents beside his plate, and was eating his way through an equally impressive spread of bacon, eggs and fried bread. He signalled to Dashwood to join him.

'How are the nasty smells coming along?'

'Getting nastier by the minute. But the guv's in a pretty cheerful mood.' Dashwood dragged a chair closer. 'Actually, he was asking how *you* were expecting to make out.'

'You can tell him later. After we've wrapped it up. He's not suddenly going to want you haring off to the docks again?'

'Not that I know of. Seems happy enough on his own for the time being.'

'Then you'd better get yourself something to eat. It's going to be a long day.'

Greig's appetite for bacon and eggs had been keen enough. He showed another, even keener appetite as he and Dashwood ushered the still uncommunicative Taylor into an interview room and closed the door. All his movements seemed exaggeratedly slow, calculated, and predatory. He went through a measured procedure of moving two chairs a fraction of an inch closer to the table, and gestured the prisoner towards one of them. Dashwood, trying to maintain the same sort of menacing pace, broke open two sealed audio cassettes and inserted one into the tape recorder on a corner table. When he had checked that the tape was running and adjusted the volume level he said deliberately and clearly: 'Melpax robbery. Interview with Eric Taylor. Those present, suspect plus Detective Sergeant Alastair Greig and myself, Detective Constable Mike Dashwood. Interview commences 10.06 a.m., Friday the nineteenth of February.'

It did show the signs, as Greig had warned, of being a long session. It was going to be a matter of hard concentration,

21

without fireworks but without let-up: a slow, slogging duel in a confined space, with remorseless questions instead of punches, the pounce on a giveaway remark, a clumsy phrase . . . if the practised, hardened Taylor could ever be trapped into giving anything whatsoever away.

Unusually Greig had chosen to place the suspect beside him instead of alone on the far side of the table. He sat at an angle, contemplating Taylor, while Dashwood took the far chair, pushing it back slightly so that it was out of Taylor's line of vision. In the silence weighing down on the three men, shut away in this bleak room, Taylor ignored the DS's gaze and stared blankly at the blank wall. Years of ugly activity had toughened his features into a pattern of unresponsiveness, not so much callous as immune to humour or harassment. He might have been quite handsome if any vestige of genuine warmth or human emotion had ever been allowed to relax those features.

At last Greig, quiet and unhurried, saw fit to comment on this. 'You look in good shape for a man of forty-eight, Eric. What's the secret?' There was no response. 'Jogging? Your local beat officer sees you out running most mornings. Not the last few days, though.' When Taylor went on staring straight ahead, he added, 'I'm sorry there are no pictures on the wall for you to look at,' and then leaned forward a fraction. 'Would you like to see a couple of Mr Redfern? The manager of the cash-and-carry, you know.'

'No,' said Taylor levelly, 'I don't know.'

Greig opened the larger of the two folders he had put on the table. Taking out a sheaf of photographs, he pushed them one by one in front of the prisoner. There was a messy one of the wound on the back of Redfern's head where he had been clubbed with a sawn-off shotgun. Next came a side angle on the blood clotting in his hair. Redfern had been let out of hospital the day before, but for a long time he would be scared to go out into the streets, or even to cross the floor of his shop. His young assistant Joanne Kelly was still under sedation. No need for a picture of her. But there was an interesting one of the doorpost, scraped by the robbers' getaway van. Then two close-ups of a patch of oil near the doorstep on which one of them had slipped – the one with the shotgun, according to Joanne, half hysterical but valiantly trying to remember details for the police. In the oil was a nice clear impression of trainer soles.

Greig looked down at Taylor's feet. 'Be about your size. And I noticed at the house this morning that your right knee's a bit puffy. Had a fall, have you?' Hardly expecting a response, he went on: 'And not one pair of trainers to be seen. Strange, that, for a man who goes jogging. Two track-suits and no trainers. Did you throw them away, Eric? Perhaps you should have dumped the trousers too. Sump oil might not show up on black but it'll still be there in the fibres. What d'you think?'

Taylor reacted at last, but only with mild self-assurance, as if politely correcting an obvious error. 'You don't get bird for having oil on your trousers. I wasn't there.' He resumed his contemplation of the wall.

'Five years ago I might have believed you, Eric.' Casually Greig opened the second folder and pretended to scan the top sheet within. 'Definitely top league then, weren't you? Would you have even looked at a scruffy little job like Melpax five years ago? Would you have teamed up with a goon like Mark Hankin?'

Mike Dashwood was sure that at the mention of Hankin's name Taylor had faintly, fractionally blinked, and wondered if the DS, looking down at the folder, had noticed. The equally faint twitch of Greig's lips suggested that he had.

Greig closed the folder. He knew it all by heart. With that disconcertingly greedy memory of his, he could swot up every essential of a dossier within less than an hour. 'We know all about you and Mark. We know that you met several times in the month before the robbery. At the Prince of Wales and at the Wheatsheaf. Hankin was on shorts, showing off. You drank lemonade as usual.' He nodded in what might have been austere teetotal approval.

'You don't get bird for that either.'

'Mark's given up the hard stuff for a while. He's drinking coffee right now. In cell three.'

Taylor grunted a brief laugh.

'You don't believe me?' Greig was on his feet, abruptly quickening the tempo. 'Okay, let's go and take a look.'

Dashwood was almost as startled as Taylor by this sudden interruption of the interview. But he managed to say: 'Mind your knee when you get up, Eric.' It won him a dourly appreciative nod from the DS as the two men went out.

In the lull Dashwood recorded the time on the tape recorder, switched off, and went back to the CID office to see if there were any messages. Crossing the custody area past the end of the cell block, he heard Greig's voice in quieter and almost reassuring mood. 'There you are, you see. I don't bull, Eric. If I tell you something, it's true. I want you to understand that.'

Dashwood went on up the stairs. He would have preferred to ignore the insistent ringing of the phone which greeted him. Somehow Greig had infected him. He wanted no interruptions to their concentration on that silent, unyielding man down in the interview room. But force of habit led him to snatch up the receiver.

It was DI Burnside, asking if there was any news yet from the hospital about old Jeffries. He wanted something positive to help him lean on Tyrone Bell at the building site. Dashwood got the impression that the DI would actually welcome news of the old man's death. Switching the conversation, Burnside certainly sounded pleased to learn that there was no news yet from the unco-operative Taylor. So Alastair was subjecting him to mild stress? It would take a lot more than that. 'Wish him luck.' It sounded gratingly insincere. 'He'll need it. Takes years to learn how to handle a pro like Taylor.'

'Still' – Mike Dashwood was unable to resist the temptation – 'he's never coughed for you, has he, guv?'

The harsh intake of breath at the other end made him suspect that he had made a bit of a mistake. Winding up

Burnside like that was no way to ensure a smooth future for himself at Sun Hill.

Detective Inspector Frank Burnside and Detective Constable Tosh Lines plodded for what must have been the tenth time across the rubble towards Tyrone Bell's portacabin. As usual, he was in the doorway before they got there, waiting for them with a mixture of truculence and apprehension.

Burnside was in a mood to enjoy himself. And he was not going to be too particular about the truth.

'I've had a really interesting piece of news from the hospital. You know the old geezer that was overcome with fumes over there, down the dock?'

'Or the cold, or whatever.'

'Or whatever,' Burnside echoed. 'It killed him, anyway,' he lied. 'Just heard from the hospital about his death, poor old sod.'

'So?'

'So you were the one who poured chemicals down the manhole. They get into a disused sewer, and an OAP gets killed. That's the sort of thing we have a nasty habit of calling manslaughter.'

'Now wait a minute – '

'I'm not waiting. I'm doing you for manslaughter.'

Bell backed away into the cabin. Tosh Lines shouldered his way in and stood beside him, ready to make a grab if necessary.

'This is crazy,' the foreman blustered. 'I ain't getting done for manslaughter just because you found a load of cleansing agent down a drain.'

Burnside smirked. 'Who said "cleansing agent"?'

'You just did.'

Burnside shook his head complacently. 'No, I didn't, Tyrone. I said "chemicals". *You* said "cleansing agent" – which is what's really down the manhole. How do you come to know that?'

Somewhere a ship hooted derisively from far along the

Thames. The note was taken up by the wail of a distant ambulance. A flurry of dust rose in a sudden swirl through the open door, and Lines coughed dryly. But if Bell, too, had a dry throat his forehead was damp and glistening.

'Mr Burnside, you're trying to put words in my mouth.'

'Oh, come on, Tyrone. I've got you. Throw in the bleedin' towel, why don't you?'

Bell sagged back against the bench under the window. 'Okay. But you got to listen to me. All right? I ain't having none of this manslaughter jive.'

'Why's that?'

''Cos it ain't me dumping it, that's why. Haven't got a lorry no more, have I, thanks to you lot.' He found time for a glare at Lines. 'I've got a mate . . . well, just a bloke I know, right? He sometimes drives a chemical lorry. I've been coming back late a couple of nights. Letting him tip a bit of cleansing agent. That's all.'

'And nothing else?'

'No. Not that I know of.'

'In that case I think maybe we ought to have a word with him. What's his name?'

'Oh, come on, man! You can't expect me to – '

'Use your noddle, old son. If you don't tell me I'll have to do you for the lot, not just for helping out.'

Bell tried to look resolute. It lasted for about twenty seconds. Breath whistled mournfully through the gap between two of his front teeth. 'Duggie Booker,' he said reluctantly. 'He works at Hughes' transfer station. You know, Terry Hughes.'

On Mike Dashwood's desk there was one newly typed sheet, right on the top of the pile. One glance was enough to show that he had the means of pleasing at any rate the DS, if not the DI. He carried it complacently with him on his return to the interview room. Alastair Greig and Eric Taylor were already back and had been joined by PC Richard Turnham, whose distant expression might have been adopted specially to disconcert the prisoner if it had not been that Turnham always looked that way. The tape was already running.

'This,' Greig was saying, 'is the officer who sees you out running in the mornings.'

'I've noticed.'

Taylor did not yet seem to be bored by the wall beyond Turnham's head.

'Your friend Mark in there was arrested yesterday,' Greig continued. 'He'll be taken to court later this morning. There'll be no trouble getting an extension of police detention.'

'Well, that's his problem.'

'I think it could be yours as well, Eric.' Greig ran a finger down the edge of the thicker folder. 'This is all evidence.'

'I thought it was bog paper.'

'Statements.'

'Not from Mark. Mark never coughs. Not ever.'

It was the first crack in Taylor's defences, and he realised it. Those words would have been better left unspoken.

Greig said: 'But Mark's careless. That's what put Baz Pocock in the frame. And Mickey Reeves. You see, Mark had left their numbers by the phone. Yours as well.' He sprawled back expansively, tilting his chair on to its two rear legs. 'As a matter of interest, how did Mickey Reeves perform? Chip off the old block? I mean, you and his dad Len used to work together.'

Taylor had relapsed into silence. Greig looked up at Mike Dashwood, still standing in the doorway. Timing it like a ponderous stage entrance, Dashwood paced forward and laid the sheet of paper on the table. Greig made an equally solemn show of studying it, then produced a knowing smile.

'Can't ask for more than that, can we?'

'Not really.' Dashwood settled himself on a chair by the wall.

Greig turned back to Taylor. 'Interesting news for you, Eric. Baz Pocock and Mickey Reeves have skipped off to Spain. Must have got wind of Mark's arrest last night. Quick off the mark, eh?' He slid the sheet along towards Taylor. 'Have a look.'

Taylor still preferred the wall.

Greig was nicely into his stride by now. 'Son Mickey and nephew Baz soaking up the sun, leaving old friend Eric to carry the can. How do you feel about that?' The pressure increased slightly. 'I thought you top villains were supposed to stick together. Or is that the point – you're not tops any more? Is that why you're in company like this little lot? Mark Hankin, Baz Pocock, Mickey Reeves, Eric Taylor . . . one brain-dead animal, two wet-arsed kids, one quality professional. And who's the one who's facing twenty years?'

'You're an optimist.'

'Eighteen minimum nowadays, Eric.'

In the reverberating silence Turnham got up and, as if sworn to observe that silence, sought a brief nod of dismissal from Greig. When he had gone, Dashwood removed the finished cassette, put another one in the recorder, recited time and sequence, and then changed chairs and faced the other two across the table.

Taylor had sagged forward, his forearms resting on his thighs. Now he was looking at the floor as intently as he had once looked at the wall.

Slowly Greig summed up the whole story. He might have been dispassionately preparing a précis for someone quite unfamiliar with the facts. Those facts were clear and brutal enough, but Taylor appeared quite unmoved by the story of the brutal attack on Redfern, or by any memory of those photographs which had been thrust under his nose. It might have happened in another city, another country, so far as he was concerned.

'And *you*,' Greig concluded, 'were the one to slip on the way out. In the oil. Dropped your gun, retrieved it, and climbed into the van as Pocock backed out. Backed out clumsily, too – gashed a fair-sized bit off the edge of the door. One dropped brick after another. Would you say that's a fair outline of events?'

28

'What time's lunch?'

Greig looked at his watch. There was too much at stake for him not to play this all according to the book. There must be no hint of police brutality, excessive pressure, or deliberate flouting of regulations. The interview was broken off for the prisoner to be escorted back to the custody area and the time of his return to the cell block duly recorded by Sergeant Penny. As Taylor walked mutely off, Penny called chirpily after him:

'Lunch is on its way, Eric. So is the police surgeon. DS Greig wants him to have a look at that knee of yours while he's here.'

After the morning's interrogation, Greig and Dashwood sat for a few fraught minutes in the interview room. Greig's need for lunch seemed non-existent. He had done all the eating he fancied today – until there was a chance of taking Taylor apart.

'All right.' It came out prickly and challenging. 'What do you think?'

'I think we all know he was there,' said Dashwood warily. 'And *he* knows you can't prove it.'

'I'll prove it. He'll tell me.'

It was too intense. The DS was staking too much on this, screwing up his nerves to snapping pitch. Trying to ease the tension, Mike Dashwood ventured: 'By the way, Burnside rang when I was upstairs earlier. He said to wish you luck.'

'You mean he hopes I fall flat on my face.'

'You know what his feelings are about Taylor.'

Greig looked down at his shoes in an eerie imitation of Taylor's pose. Then his head jerked up. 'And what about you, Mike?' It was a clear demand to know where the DC stood.

'Me? Well . . . I'm in the middle, aren't I?'

'Good for you.' It was the first sign of bitterness Greig had allowed himself to show. But then, like Burnside, he was learning there was plenty to be bitter about.

Mike Dashwood went off for a lunch which he failed to enjoy. This afternoon was going to be one hell of an afternoon; and the end of it would be even more hellish if Taylor sat tight and refused to crack.

Three

Sergeant Penny stooped to pick up the lunch tray from the cell floor. He was on his way out of the cell when Greig appeared, propping himself against the jamb of the open door.

'Lunch any good?'

'No,' said Taylor.

Greig mimed mild surprise. 'Sorry to hear that. I think the food here isn't too bad on the whole. Better than prison anyway. But then, it's a long time since you've tried that, isn't it? 1979.' He sounded impressed. 'Not many armed robbers go ten years without a conviction. Not ten active years.'

Taylor said: 'Frank Burnside usually closes the door.'

'I like it open. The Custody Officer's outside. Shout if you feel oppressed.' Greig took matches and a packet of cigarettes from his jacket pocket and tossed them to Taylor, who automatically and expertly caught both of them; then glowered at the speed of his own reaction. Without acknowledgment he took out a cigarette and lit up. 'I was surprised to find out you smoke,' said Greig as if this somehow scored a point.

'Nobody's perfect.'

'Oh, and did the surgeon give you any liniment for your knee?'

'Hadn't got a clue.'

There was a pause while Taylor inhaled, looked at one of the cell walls, and decided this was not worthy of his attention. He blew a smoke ring towards the barred window.

'I had the feeling,' Greig invited, 'that you might want to talk, off the record.'

31

'I can't help you. Sorry.'

'I appreciate it's difficult. Obviously you've got things to consider.'

'It's difficult,' Taylor agreed, 'because I wasn't there.'

Greig let that ride for a moment, then said: 'You don't like prison, do you, Eric?'

'Who does?'

'But you like it less than most. A bit beneath your dignity, isn't it?'

In the background somebody in the custody area was shouting abuse, and Sergeant Cryer's competent voice was issuing instructions. Somewhere a door slammed. Footsteps went along the corridor of the cell block, paused, and went on. Greig idly swung the door of Taylor's cell to and fro, a few inches at a time.

'Eric, if you don't plead to this and you're found guilty, it'll be top whack, no question. You don't need me to tell you that.'

'Don't tell me, then.'

'We can't hang around here for ever.'

'Like I said, I can't help you.'

'Why's that? Scared?'

That triggered off an angry response. 'Who of?'

'Mark Hankin?' Leaving time for Taylor's grunt of contempt, Greig proceeded: 'The Reeves family, then? But no one else is going to blame you for talking, not after the way they've cut and run. You'd have nothing to fear from the likes of them, Eric. Or from their friends, if they've got any. Nor would your family. Arrangements can be made.'

Taylor reacted again. 'I'll look after my family, not you. All right?'

Greig had found a nerve, and went gently and repeatedly for it. 'I was admiring the photos at the house this morning. Son fourteen, the girl twelve, mm? Graeme and Jolie. You still see a lot of them, I believe . . . though you and Linda are divorced.'

'You are one nosey git.'

'What bait did you use to catch the carp?'

Momentarily thrown, Taylor glared suspiciously. 'Do what?' He lit a second cigarette from the fading glow of the first.

'The father-and-son fishing trophy in the lounge. Twenty-pound carp.'

'Oh, that. Sweet corn.'

'Pity you didn't wait for Graeme to grow up a bit.' Greig was keeping it casual. 'You could have taken him on the job. He wouldn't have dropped you in it like Mickey.'

'You leave Graeme out of this.' The nerve that Greig had probed was twitching more and more violently. 'He's clean.'

'I know he is. Both your kids are. I've checked.'

'Then shut up about them. Stuff it.'

'Do your kids know how you make a living, Eric? Graeme could only have been a year old when you were last sent down. Jolie wasn't even born. Have you stashed away enough for them to live on? Not from Melpax you haven't.' Greig waited, his breath dry in his throat. He gave it a long two minutes. 'There's nothing you want to say to me, then?'

Taylor was looking past him into the corridor: not planning to make a dash for it; just looking; or maybe carefully not looking at anything at all.

'All right.' Greig shrugged. 'If you want to draw out the agony, I've still got oceans of time before I have to charge you, and the forensic's coming in all the while. If that's the way you want to leave it, that's the way it'll have to be. You're the one facing twenty years and no family. I'm the one with the evidence.'

'Evidence? You've got no poxy evidence.'

Greig pushed himself away from the door. 'I'll tell it to the tape recorder when I'm good and ready. You don't have to listen, okay?'

As he stepped aside, Sergeant Penny came along rattling the cell keys. Taylor took a quick drag at the cigarette he had recently started, and tossed it on the floor. Penny carefully trod on the smouldering butt and picked up the matches and packet from the bench. He made the cell door clang shut particularly loudly as he left.

It was the first time, he confided to Mike Dashwood in passing, that he had ever known Taylor waste a cigarette. So, Dashwood insinuated, would he be prepared to take bets on the outcome of the interrogation?

'I'm not a betting man,' said Penny.

'Personally, I think Greig's going to crack before Taylor does.'

Dashwood went back to the CID office, and was on the phone, jotting down notes, when Greig came in and watched sourly, as if suspecting him of giving Burnside a malicious update. In fact the details coming through were a preliminary forensic report on the trousers. They added up, at best, to a definite maybe: similar oil, similar grains of dust, similar particles of metal; but not what you'd call substantial evidence. Nor was there any report on the gloves yet. He put the phone down and summed up for Greig's benefit.

'It'll do,' said Greig.

'Not for a good defence barrister, it won't.'

'We're not addressing a good defence barrister,' said Greig tartly. 'We're addressing a man who knows he was involved in a messy job, who knows he couldn't survive twenty years inside, and who knows that I've got every minute detail about him right.'

The overstatement stung Mike Dashwood to protest. 'It seems to me we're very long on research and still short on proof.'

'What about Vince Carter?'

'SO8 aren't saying yet. In any event, even if – '

'Even if, even if . . . What's your problem, Mike?'

'*My* problem?'

'Shall I get someone else to sit in for the rest of the session? Let you get back to Burnside and the sweet smell of old sewage? That might be less tedious for you.'

'No.' Dashwood restrained himself with difficulty from shouting. 'Of course I want to stay on this case.'

34

'Well, start being a bit more positive, right?'

They went downstairs in hostile silence. Taylor was escorted back into the interview room, and the three settled themselves in their respective chairs. This time, however, Taylor chose to lean his right elbow on the table, resting his chin on his hand. He was no longer quite as still as before. His left hand picked a couple of times at the edge of the table, removing stains or splinters that were not there.

Greig nudged one of his folders at an angle as if inviting the prisoner to read a few selections from it.

'The police surgeon says the bruising to your knee is definitely consistent with a recent fall on something hard. Like a concrete floor. What do you say about that, Eric?'

'Is that the best you've got?'

'Why, does that make a difference to your answer?' asked Greig keenly. 'I mean, if you didn't hurt your knee at Melpax, when did you hurt it? Where's the harm in telling me that?'

'I don't give alibis. I don't need them.'

'I'm only trying to establish the truth.'

'You try what you like, you can't establish a thing.' Taylor sat back and folded his arms. 'Because I wasn't there.'

Greig regarded him for a long moment. Dashwood wondered whether he had run out of ideas. Then Greig said: 'Why do you fold your arms when you say you weren't there? Did it this morning too, I noticed.'

'I never . . . it's got nothing to do with . . .'

'I think you do it when you're lying, Eric. You've been telling me just that one lie all day. Just the one. So that would be very easy to rectify, wouldn't it? Not a major climb-down at all.'

Taylor unfolded his arms, then defiantly folded them again. When Greig took a sheet of paper from the folder, it was met with a weary little snort.

'Not the bog paper again.'

'The oil on your tracksuit trousers has now been analysed. Metal filaments and grains of concrete dust found in it closely match those found in a sample taken from the patch of oil at

Melpax. What's your view on that?' When Taylor shrugged, Greig said in a voice as chill as a sea wind along his native Scottish coast: 'If folding your arms means you're lying, what does shrugging mean – that you're beginning to see sense?'

'It means it's time you gave it a rest.'

Greig glanced at his watch. 'We've hardly started. Plenty of time till next review. Look, I don't think you quite appreciate what you're up against, Eric. It's not just me and DC Dashwood in this room. The whole investigative machinery of the Met has clicked into gear on this case. And I must say you and your mates did leave us so much to go on. The next piece of "bog paper" I'm expecting is about your gloves.' He tried another long pause, while Dashwood shifted in his chair. His back was beginning to ache. 'Do you remember,' asked Greig, 'what Joanne, the young girl at the cash-and-carry, was wearing? When you grabbed her and stuck the shotgun in her face?' He had hardly expected a response. 'She was wearing a red woollen sweater. And minute fibres of red wool from that will have attached themselves to your gloves.'

'I've got a red sweater at home. I keep it in the same drawer as my gloves.'

'Yours is a Pringle. Hers is Marks and Spencer.'

Taylor seemed to consult the floor on this, then looked calmly into Greig's face. 'Have you any idea how many red M-and-S sweaters there are in the world – Alastair?'

'A lot. But not so many in each colour batch. You know that each red batch is slightly different, do you? Which cuts down the chance of coincidence an awful lot.' Greig leaned forward. 'It was a big mistake to grab the girl, Eric. One dropped brick after another, eh? And as we pick them up we build a wall. And in the end we'll have no choice but to brick you up completely. For twenty years.' His voice had gone very, very quiet. 'If that's what you want.'

Taylor began picking at his teeth, and examined his finger-nail reflectively.

The atmosphere was becoming claustrophobic. Dashwood could feel Greig beginning to scent a possible kill. For himself, he would be glad to get it over with. On the whole he wondered if he might have done better to accept the chance of rejoining Burnside in the open air, no matter how much that air might stink.

The yard behind the high-wire fence and the huddle of brick buildings and chimneys formed a typical dockland collection and holding station for industrial solids and chemical waste. Here there were safe, officially approved processes for storing and methodically disposing of chemicals according to a strict set of regulations. Lines swung the car around two lorries unloading beside a bay with wide doors pulled back, and came to a halt outside another portacabin. A man in overalls was coming out – overalls cleaner than Tyrone Bell's, and a face that was more commanding and less shifty than Bell's.

'Can I help you?'

'Probably, chief.' Tosh Lines showed his warrant card and did the talking. 'CID, Sun Hill. Is Mr Hughes about?'

'That's me.'

'We're looking for a driver of yours. Duggie Booker.'

'Duggie?' The man might not have looked as shifty as Bell at first, but his evasive glance at one of the lorries by the bay suggested he could well be a senior member of the same league. 'He's not here at the moment.'

A driver jumped up into the cab of the nearest lorry and began backing out. Lines was a heavy man, overweight but in deceptively good condition. It took him six strides to reach the lorry and make a leap for its footplate.

'Just a minute, sir.' He clung on as the lorry swung wildly towards the gate. 'Switch off, please.'

'I'm in a hurry.'

'So are we. Police. Turn it off!'

They jolted to a standstill, and the driver cut the ignition. Tosh leaned across him to pick some paperwork from the dashboard. The name of Douglas Booker was clear enough across the top of the loading sheet. Lines gestured that he should climb down. Resignedly, Booker slouched across beside Lines to the other two men.

'Sorry,' Hughes was babbling. 'Didn't realise he was in. What's he done?'

'That's what we're trying to find out, sir.'

Burnside added: 'And we'd like you to come down to Sun Hill station for a little chat, if you don't mind.'

'Are you nicking me?' Hughes demanded.

'No – why? Done something wrong?'

A plate of biscuits and three plastic cups of tea had been set on the table of the interview room. Eric Taylor was moodily sipping at his tea. Greig seemed to have recovered some of his appetite, and was visibly enjoying his third biscuit. Dashwood was glad of the interval, but wondered how long the DS was going to prolong it.

It was Taylor who broke the silence. 'There were some fags about earlier. Any chance of having one?'

'Smoking creates a terrible fug in this room, Eric.' Greig set his empty cup back on the table. 'I'd rather you didn't, if you don't mind.'

'I wish you'd stop being so bloody polite.'

'I was well brought up. Like your kids.'

'Shut it.'

'If you go down for twenty years,' said Greig sadly, 'Graeme'll be thirty-four by the time you get out. A middle-aged man. What's he going to turn out like, without a father?'

'I told you to shut it.'

Greig was really moving in now. 'The truth always has to be faced in the end. And that's all I want from you, Eric, the truth.'

Taylor rubbed his hands together, shook his head several times, and laughed jerkily. 'I still don't think you've got enough.'

'What do you mean by that? That you were at the robbery but you'll walk away from it. Is that what you're saying?'

'No, that's not what I'm saying. What d'you think I am, stupid?'

'You're an intelligent man. So why use the word "enough"? If you weren't there, what does it matter how much evidence I've got? You know I won't fit you up, so what are you worried about?'

Taylor's head drooped. 'I'm due a break.'

'No, you're not, actually. But,' said Greig gently, 'you can have one. Give you a chance for some right thinking, Eric. Okay?'

Dashwood got up, lurching because his left leg was threatening to go to sleep, and went to call two PCs to escort the prisoner back to his cell. When Taylor had gone, head bowed wearily, Dashwood waited for Greig to collect his folders.

'Is that true about the colour batches?'

'Yes,' said Greig curtly. 'I'm long on research. You said so yourself.'

He strode away. Dashwood hurried to catch him up. 'Alastair. I am on your side, you know.'

Greig nodded impassively. 'What I could do with is confirmation on the gloves. And something definite from SO8 on Carter would be nice.'

Dashwood took the hint and went off to the CID office to put through a couple of calls. One of them bore fruit. He hurried back downstairs and found Greig in the washroom, sluicing his face and then carefully combing his hair. By the time they resumed work in the interview room he looked neat and fresh; which was more than Dashwood felt, and more than could be said for Taylor, by now seeming to shrink in on himself.

'Sorry to have left you on your own for so long, Eric,' said Greig amiably. 'Continuing enquiries, you understand. But at least it'll have given you plenty of time to think things over. So, is there anything you think you'd like to say to me?'

Taylor remained hunched up in his chair. Again he was rubbing his hands slowly, almost hypnotically, together.

Greig let it ride for a while, then abruptly said, 'What made you use a different armourer this time?'

Taylor's hands froze. Slowly he looked up.

'Couldn't you afford the top prices any more? Is that why you went to Vince Carter?' Pressing home the surprise, Greig explained: 'He was lifted this morning. Been questioned most of the day. He says that you picked up and returned the happy bag yourself.'

'He's a poxy liar.'

'He's a criminal, Eric. Making choices, just like you. Only he hasn't got much stamina. He's chosen to tell the truth and get it over with. Very bright of him.'

Taylor turned unexpectedly towards Dashwood as if hoping for confirmation. 'Vince Carter? *Truth*? He wouldn't even be able to spell the word. He's got more convictions than . . .' Breath exploded from him in a great shuddering gust. 'Go on, stick him up in court then, and see what my brief does to him.'

'I don't think I'll have to stick him up in court. One of his shotguns has a damaged stock. I expect examination will reveal that it's been dropped on concrete recently. And further examination will reveal traces of Mr Redfern's scalp. Remember? Where you hit him. And then all we have to find is the tiniest trace of you on it. It was such a messy job we're bound to find something. Doesn't matter how microscopic.' Greig stared at Taylor, willing him to return the gaze. 'Would you still fancy your chances then? I tell you, I fancy mine. Wool . . . oil . . . gun. You're nearly bricked up. All *you* can decide is how long for.'

Taylor rubbed his face with both hands, then stood up. Dashwood turned wearily on his chair as Taylor went and leaned against the wall, his forehead pressed against it. Suddenly he turned and kicked his chair into the edge of the table. It bounced back and fell on its side, but before Dashwood could get up, Taylor was back against the wall. Greig remained seated, unperturbed, waiting.

'Think of your kids, Eric.'

'Stop playing games!' raged Taylor. Then it rasped out of him, 'What are you offering?'

Greig did not blink. 'Nothing. But you know you can trust me. Everything possible would be done.'

'That's not definite enough.'

'I'm not making promises I can't keep. Only two things are certain: denial could mean twenty years; getting it off your chest means a lot less.'

There was a resonant, interminable silence. Taylor did not turn away from the wall, but at last he said very quietly: 'How much less? Single figures?'

Greig got up and set Taylor's chair back on its legs. He glanced at the tape recorder to be sure it was still running, and went back to his own chair.

'In your own time, Eric.'

Four

Burnside was looking fairly well pleased with himself as two uniformed PCs escorted the surly Terry Hughes and Duggie Booker across the custody area to the desk. Sergeant Penny booked them in while Tosh Lines fidgeted, impatient for the formalities to be over.

'Right,' said Burnside. 'I'll take Mr Hughes. And Tosh, I'm sure you can rely on some friendly co-operation from Mr Booker.' He glanced at Penny. 'Interview rooms free? Or is Alastair still sweating it out in there?'

'Alastair finished not ten minutes ago.' Tom Penny allowed himself a sidelong smile at nobody in particular. 'He got what he wanted.'

'You mean . . .'

'Eric Taylor. All wrapped up.'

Burnside took it with the stoicism of a hard-muscled man receiving a rugger ball in a sensitive part of his anatomy. 'I'd better go and pat him on the head. Keep Mr Taylor somewhere comfortable for a few minutes, right?'

He stamped off towards the CID office, knowing that behind his back Penny and Lines would be swapping comments about him, and knowing pretty well what the tone of those comments would be.

Mike Dashwood was at his desk, tidying up a few papers between intermittent yawns.

'Alastair not here?'

'Just nipped down to the canteen, guv. He felt in need of a pot of tea to soothe his throat. And a few rock buns, to celebrate, you might say.'

'Yeh. I might. From what I hear. Right, then. Since you're

42

no longer needed to hold his hand, I want you over at the transfer station.'

'But guv, I've been at it all day. It's time I was . . .'

'Time you were over at that yard. Because Madame Curie is on her way there, and she'll get pretty mad if there isn't a welcoming committee on the spot for her.'

It was not the time to argue. Not with Burnside knotting up his face into a congratulatory smile and trying to look as if he meant it, as he went off to the canteen in search of DS Greig. Somebody had to suffer just to make up for that goodwill mission. Mike stifled another yawn and hauled himself wearily to his feet.

In the interview room Lines opened his notebook. He hoped he could repeat the triumph which Alastair Greig had achieved in here today. Maybe there would still be some inspiring waves or echoes left on the air.

Duggie Booker took a nervous pull at a cigarette. Lines had every intention of keeping him nervous.

'Not very clever of you trying to drive out of Hughes' yard with a police officer hanging off your lorry, Duggie.'

'I wasn't to know who you were, was I?'

'Oh, you do disappoint me. I thought you blokes could smell a copper a mile off.'

'Only if the wind's in the right direction.'

'You're looking a little worried, Duggie. Guess you know why you're here?'

'I ain't worried. But I think I've got a right to know what this is all about.'

'I'm not telling. Just waiting for you to tell *me*.'

Duggie looked round at the tape recorder in the corner of the room. 'Aren't you supposed to use that in all your interviews nowadays?'

'What for? I thought we were only having a little chat. Anyway, I haven't charged you with anything. So far.' Lines made a great show of writing several lines on his pad, aware that Booker was dying to know what they contained. Not

43

very good at feigning indifference, was chunky-shouldered but muddled-up Duggie. 'I'm going to offer you a deal, Duggie. You tell me what you know I know already, and I'll make sure your co-operation goes down on my statement. Look good in court if I put in a word for you. And believe me, mate, you're going to need a few friends in there.'

'On your bike. I ain't done nothing.'

'You're sticking to that?'

'Course I am.'

'Please yourself. In that case I'm arresting you on suspicion of illegally disposing of chemical products.' Tosh Lines snapped his notebook shut and took a cassette from his pocket. 'Now you can really start worrying, Duggie.'

He wondered how Burnside was making out with Booker's boss in the charge room.

The DI, having delivered himself of some well-phrased praise for Greig's achievement, was in fact very much in the mood for getting that out of his system by making somebody else's life as miserable as was humanly, or inhumanely, possible. Notebook in hand, as burly as Lines but a whole lot more threatening, he was saying:

'You see, Mr Hughes, I'm not up on chemicals, but apparently someone's been dumping a cleansing agent near Minister Wharf.'

'Silly of them. But what's that got to do with me?'

'Didn't I mention that?' said Burnside guilelessly. 'You did it. That's what it's got to do with you. Or should I say you paid Duggie Booker to do it?'

'Crap.'

'It's killed someone, you know.'

Hughes stared, framing an indignant response; then, pale, kept his mouth shut. Something was worse than he had thought it was going to be.

Burnside said: 'You do process bleach and acid, right?'

'You know that.'

'Which mixed together can be lethal.'

'What's this, anyway – guilt by association?'

'Ooh, that's a good phrase. I must remember that.'

Dashwood appeared suddenly at Burnside's shoulder. He looked even more weary than he had looked before. 'Guv, she's here.'

Burnside scowled, then turned it swiftly to his own use. 'Right, Terry. Now we're going to find out where you got that acid.'

'You'll have a job.'

'Got plenty of time, have you?'

'I wanna brief.'

Burnside ignored this and followed Mike Dashwood across the custody area. 'Anything useful?'

'Not really, guv.'

'Then what you brought her back here for?'

Dashwood, who had obviously had a gruelling half-hour, said with malicious respectfulness: 'I think she'd like a few words.'

'Lucky me. Where is she, then?'

'I left her in the corridor. Everywhere else seems overcrowded.'

The corridor leading to the station yard was not the most comfortable place for a visitor. The outer door swung intermittently to and fro to admit PCs, WPCs, and draughts. Men clattering down the stairs from the upper floor tended to put a hand on the rail at the bottom and spin round the corner to collide with anyone careless enough to be standing near by. Dr Jane Reece's lean, analytical features looked as if she had made a careful diagnosis of Burnside's character and was prepared to classify it along with other dangerous irritants for which a very powerful antidote was urgently required. She gave him no time to make any soothing or welcoming noises.

'What exactly was the meaning of dragging me away from the docks and rushing me off to that transfer station?'

'I was rather hoping you'd find me some conclusive evidence, doctor.'

'If I'm to be forced to work for you, then please allow me to do so in my own logical way.'

Viv Martella and June Ackland brushed past, carefully not looking at the visitor's harshly critical face but enjoying the sound of her harshly critical voice directed against the DI.

'Doctor, was there any acid there? That's what I was after.'

'None. Did you expect to find the two together?'

'We were rather hoping so.'

'Hm. You will learn, inspector, that life is never that simple. Even if I found anything toxic it wouldn't mean the stuff in the dockyard came from the transfer station.'

'No, but I did think maybe – '

'You do realise that whatever laid that pensioner out could be killing people at the site now? I ought to be there finding out where the fumes came from, not whose fault it is. That's *your* job.'

'And that's the job I'm trying to do. With your assistance.'

'I don't have time to waste gallivanting round transfer stations. Or standing in this awful building. If you'll let me get back to the docks – '

'Doctor!' Burnside advanced a menacing step. 'In an interview room just through there, I have a suspect who might hear every word you're saying. If you continue to shout your mouth off, two things may happen. Firstly, you may allow him to become party to information I would not wish him to hear. And secondly, I may charge you under the Noise Abatement Act.'

Dashwood turned away and pretended to be studying a section of the yard visible through the glass of the outer door.

Dr Reece stiffened. 'Very well. I'm sorry.' She was subdued but still steady and dignified. 'But I was not shouting.'

'Let's call it a subdued bellow, then. Look, I'm sorry we sent you down to Hughes' yard on a bum steer. But I have to try everything. I'm desperately in need of enough evidence to charge those cowboys before they realise they could just get up and walk out.'

'In that case, get me back to the building site and I may just get it for you.'

46

'Certainly. Dashwood' – this would wipe the grin off the DC's face – 'take Dr Reece back to the site.'

The search took longer than they had anticipated. It was not until dusk, when Mike Dashwood was beginning to wonder if this day would ever end, that the fire brigade made a breakthrough. They had cordoned off the area around the manhole and made several descents into the sewers with breathing apparatus. Dr Reece had sent for a dye which could be poured into side pipes from the main drain and which would, hopefully, appear from the outflow into the river. It frustratingly failed to do so; in which case it must be taking its time tracing out a lethal path somewhere else.

'If it gets any darker,' the doctor grumbled, 'we won't be able to see anything anyway. Yet I would have sworn . . .'

A fireman appeared unexpectedly alongside the skip where Gertie had been found, like a duck which had submerged only to bob up again several yards away. He waved to his mates. In a matter of minutes they had kicked and shovelled rubble aside, and helped him lever up the remains of a heavy wooden flap, rotting away round the edges.

The fire officer came sliding down the slope to Reece and Dashwood.

'There's an old cellar there. Part of one of these buildings they've been demolishing. Stuff in there that must have been buried for ages.'

The next ten minutes of cautious exploration seemed to be the longest part of the whole operation. Dr Reece's face became animated. She could not bear to wait for the revelation of what lay beneath the wilderness of the building site. Dashwood felt a tingle of anticipation himself; but even more acutely felt the urge to go off duty and put his feet up.

When another of the firemen finally emerged and came down to present her with an old, corroded label, Dr Reece was transformed into a quite different woman. She began to pace round the cordoned-off area, and would probably have been quite unperturbed if the ground opened and swallowed her up, provided it confirmed her theories.

It was all pretty clear now. The area was honeycombed with old cellars. And one of them was right under the skip where PC Haynes had reported the old woman's corpse. In it were old drums of cyanide and hypochlorine. Even from this distance there was a tang of it, newly released into the open air, faintly burning at the back of Dashwood's throat. The cleansing agent dumped down the manhole had been running steadily into a cracked, disused sewer which in turn flooded into the cellars.

'And there,' said the doctor triumphantly, 'it mixed with the cyanide and ran along the sewer into the river, and began killing off your old age pensioner. It all makes sense: the fastest piece of detective work today,' she gloated.

'So how come Haynes wasn't affected when he was with the tramp – the old woman?'

'Because that one didn't die of cyanide poisoning. *She* was killed by chlorine gas. The cyanide gas is heavier: it went straight down to the river. The chlorine gas must have seeped up through the cellar roof. It only kills in a confined space, which is what the poor old girl created when she tucked herself into that shelter and tried to seal herself in.' Dr Reece looked around the blighted landscape, sour realisation beginning to embitter her jubilation. 'Some of these cellars must be like time bombs waiting to go off. One idiot fly-tipping, that's all it takes. I hope you lot throw the book at him.'

'If you'd like to come back with me to Sun Hill,' said Dashwood, 'maybe we can find out how the guv'nor's making out in that direction.'

The smoke in the interview room had built up into a fug which would have displeased Alastair Greig's austere nose. Tosh Lines was quite happy with it. The speed with which Duggie Booker was ditching one fag in order to grope for another spoke volumes . . . or tape cassettes.

'Come on, Duggie. It's a losing battle and you know it. We

48

know you've been dumping chemicals. What I don't know is why you're holding out.'

'Chemicals, me? No way you could believe that.'

'Your mate and mine, Tyrone Bell, has told us.'

'I don't fall for that one.'

'He told us,' Tosh perservered, 'because, unlike you and your chum Hughes, Bell has a conscience. He didn't realise those chemicals were toxic. Mug that he was, he went ahead thinking they were harmless.'

'Don't be stupid.'

'And when toxic chemicals get into the river they start screwing up the environment. And eventually killing people. Which is what you've done, Duggie.'

'Don't give me that.'

'This afternoon an old man died from inhaling the fumes you caused. I think we could call that manslaughter.'

'I ain't killed nobody.' The cigarette trembled between Booker's fingers, and ash fell on to his knee. 'I'm a lorry driver, not Charles Manson.'

'So tell me the truth about the chemicals, then.'

Duggie Booker flapped a despondent hand. 'Okay. I did dump some cleansing agent. But that's all it was. Not toxic. Unless Hughes has been chucking something else in, without telling me.'

Lines tried to keep very solemn and not betray himself by too joyful a smirk. Once they started trying to shift things to someone else, you'd got them – in this case, with a bit of luck, both of them. 'He's in on it as well, is he?' he asked, almost offhandedly.

'Too right he is. Look, if I'm going down, he's coming down with me. He's been charging people the going rate for safe disposal, and bunging me and Bell a ton for dumping it. Saves him loads, it does.'

'Now we're getting somewhere.' Lines stood up and switched off the tape recorder. 'Have a break, Duggie. Got enough fags left?'

He went along to the charge room, knocked and put his

head round the door, jerking his head at Burnside in a wordless signal. Treating Hughes to a hard stare as if to pin him down where he sat, Burnside added a warning nod to the PC in the third chair, got up, and came out into the corridor.

'Well?'

'Doing nicely on the manslaughter line. Booker's dead scared. He's trying to spread the load. Just starting to drop wheeler-dealer Hughes in it. Thought you'd like to know.'

'Good. And I can tell you something so you can needle him with a clear conscience. Even high-falutin' Alastair wouldn't kick against this one. Just had word the poor old geezer's really packed it in. So the manslaughter's on the cards all right if we can stick 'em for the acid and all. Keep going, Tosh. And now, back to Mr Hughes.'

Burnside went to collect a batch of statement forms, and returned to the charge room. He nodded benevolently at the PC. 'Two teas, please, John.' When the uniformed officer had gone, he flipped the form onto the table in front of Hughes. 'Gotcha! I expect you've got a novel in you just waiting to flood out.'

Hughes' pasty face twisted in flabby protest at the DI's aggressive tone. 'Are you a nutter or something?'

'No, not me. I'm not the one who goes around killing people. Not officially, anyway. No, we're witnessing what they call the domino effect, Terry.'

'You what?'

'Bell shops Booker. Booker shops you. Only who have *you* got left to shop? Wicked world, isn't it? Mind you, you've held out the longest, so that means I can be nastier to you than the others.'

It was all too clear that he meant it. Terry Hughes said: 'I wanna brief.' It was a cry all too familiar within the Sun Hill precincts, usually signifying that the end was not too far off.

'I ain't charged you yet. Now listen. Duggie's told us you only dumped some cleansing agent. And something about the way he told it – something about all that shaking and crying, probably – makes us think he was telling the truth. So that's half the puzzle solved. What you've got to tell me is this: who dumped the acid for you?'

'No one.'

'Don't tell me you dumped it yourself? That's very naughty, you know.'

He had been expecting Hughes to crack any minute; yet somehow the man was holding on, with a remarkably convincing expression of puzzled indignation. He had more stamina than you would have thought, to look at him.

'I didn't dump it at all.'

'All right, Terry. You're a hard one all right, I'll grant you that. Which means, unhappily for you, that you're the number one contestant for the accidental fall down our station stairs.'

'You really are a nutter.'

'Well, that makes two of us, then. When did you tip the acid in the sewer, Terry?'

'I didn't.'

'Don't lie.' Burnside was shouting now. He leaned over Hughes. 'You go on lying and I warn you, you'll only get me going.'

There was a tap at the door. This time it was Mike Dashwood, looking tired but a trifle smug. Burnside closed the charge room door warily behind him, but kept his hand on the knob.

Dashwood said: 'We've just solved the mystery of the acid.'

'That makes two of us. Hughes is just about to give me a nice little confession, I fancy.'

'About dumping the acid?'

'Any minute now.'

'But he didn't.'

'What the hell have you been . . .'

'He didn't, guv. We found some barrels of cyanide. And they're years old.'

Burnside digested this. He seemed to find the taste displeasing, but then smiled sourly. 'I must be more persuasive than I thought. I've just spent an hour and a half convincing him he dumped it.'

'Not at Minister Wharf he didn't.'

'Oh, dear. Some people'll say anything to get rid of me. Tell you what, Mike. Go flap those statement forms in there around for a while, and then find out what he really has dumped. Not that it'll alter things a lot. CPS permitting, I've decided to have a go for manslaughter anyway.'

Dashwood stared resentfully. 'So it doesn't matter about the cyanide and stuff?'

'Maybe, maybe not.'

'So I've been running round like a blue-arsed fly with that old dragon for nothing?'

Burnside shrugged. Then, with a flicker of curiosity, he asked: 'Where *was* the stuff, then?'

'In some cellars, right under the skip.'

'Right under the body?'

'Sir.'

'Didn't any of you dozy pillocks think of looking?'

'No.' Dashwood had had more than enough for one day. '*You* didn't, sir!'

'Brilliant. Bet old Marie Curie loved that.'

'I think you could say she had a field day, guv.' Dashwood took great pleasure in adding, in an undertone: 'She's right behind you.'

Burnside swung round as the door to the yard swung shut behind Dr Reece and she came marching along the corridor. He summoned up a sketch of a smile and went to meet her. It was the second time today that he had had to force out some form of congratulation; and it was going to be even less agreeable than the first time.

Five

There were dull mornings, dangerous mornings, awkward mornings, and downright infuriating mornings. There could be especially exasperating Monday mornings. Or there could be a certain relief in coming back from a weekend with squalling kids and a wife in a twitchy mood because her mother had been at her again, or a weekend spent golfing with local dignitaries to whom one had to be politer than they deserved. This Monday offered a fair selection.

It was a sunny day, which was a bonus after a wet Sunday afternoon and evening. Pete Ramsey and June Ackland started out in a good, relaxed mood, cruising around in search not so much for trouble as for something mildly entertaining to occupy the opening hours of the week. Nobody was yet wide awake enough to be snatching handbags outside the supermarket. The weekend's petty villains were either sleeping it off or tactfully shifting their proceeds out of the way. A dodgy-looking van starting out from a side street behind a boarded-up radio shop seemed a good enough way of filling in the time. Ramsey pursued it at a leisurely pace around two gasometers and a scrapyard, then chose a wide stretch of road to overtake and flag the driver down. Briskly he ordered the man out. There was no argument, just a weary curl of the lip and an automatic reaching for the vehicle documents, as if this was a routine happening every day, every hour on the hour.

June wandered round to open a rear door and found the interior disappointingly empty. The documents were in order, but contained no mention of a pretty obvious colour change. The sheer emptiness of the vehicle worried June, though she

53

could not have explained why innocence on a Monday morning should be just as disturbing to a trained policewoman's eye as violent guilt on a Saturday night.

'All right,' said Ramsey. 'By rights I should have traffic patrol out here to examine this bit of scrap and see about having it taken off the road. But I'm feeling good today. Usually I don't like Mondays.'

As the van creaked and spluttered away, June opened her door of the panda car and said, puzzled: 'We might have questioned him a bit further. There was something dodgy there: something about the whole feel of it.'

'Look, June. If we're going to get a job, let's at least get a half-decent one.' Ramsey slid into the driver's seat. 'Something with a bit of meat on, hey?'

'You mean something where there's an insurance payout?'

'Now you're thinking positive.'

They drove away, reasonably amicable, reasonably unperturbed. The sun was still shining, and a pale haze over the tattered playground of a housing estate made it look almost picturesque. Nothing too nasty was looming over the horizon. Not so far.

Bob Cryer showed up unexpectedly in the sergeants' office, although it was his day off.

'Thought you were off.' Sergeant Alec Peters looked over his desk. 'Long weekend, wasn't it? Can't bear to keep your nose out of things?'

Cryer scratched the long beak of his bony nose ruefully. 'Had to pick up some NHS forms.'

'Not having a truss fitted, are you?'

Cryer had another tap at his nose and grudgingly confessed that he was due for an examination and a prescription for spectacles. Peters, his own eyes for many years hidden behind glasses, found this very cheering: a sign of maturity, or maybe impending decrepitude, in the long-lasting, tough old father-figure of Sun Hill.

Business cranked up as shoppers went down the high street

and into the mall. Monday morning motorists with hangovers swerved the odd inch too far to the right, or stopped halfway into a yellow box at the crossroads. Somebody tried to mug an old lady in a back alley only to find that she had been to ju-jitsu classes. Then came the quiet introduction to a rather unusual situation – an unusually embarrassing one, for Monday or any other morning.

There was no record in Sun Hill archives of an officer having ever been called in to stop a fellow copper's wife creating a disturbance in a bank; and it was not the most enjoyable assignment any of them would have relished at any time, let alone within a few hours of coming on duty at the beginning of the week.

At first the full awkwardness did not dawn on Viv Martella, who had taken the call and was relaying the information to PCs Smith and Edwards.

'A disturbance at the London Capital Bank in Townsend Road.'

'A hold-up?'

'Don't get too brave, boys. Just somebody arguing about their account. And the manager's at his wits' end – just can't get the woman out or make her keep her voice down.'

Taffy Edwards grimaced at Yorkie Smith. 'Some woman, boyo. Any bank manager raises his eyebrow at me, and I'm off as fast as can be, and keeping my voice very much down.'

They moved along, round the corner, in no great hurry. Women arguing with their bank managers could hardly pose much of a threat, unless they started chucking heavy gold bars to and fro.

It was only when they were shown into the manager's office that the awful truth hit Yorkie. He whispered something, more to himself than to Taffy. But Edwards had already seen. The two of them slowed their pace to an even more reluctant crawl. At one till, where a cashier was hurriedly putting up a 'Closed' notice in spite of the earliness of the hour, a woman was trying to argue first with the retreating clerk and then with the manager who had come round the

55

end of the counter. Two small children were sitting on the edge of the counter, kicking their heels fretfully against the woodwork, while a third plucked at his mother's skirt. The woman, raising her voice to repeat what she had obviously said several times before without success, was in her late twenties and had straw-blonde hair which could have been smart and gleaming had it not become so unkempt, and a pale, pretty face with half-closed eyes which could have been drowsily alluring if their corners were not so creased with worry. She was, unmistakably, close to blowing her top. She was, also unmistakably, the wife of Detective Constable Alfred Lines.

Edwards winced, and looked at Yorkie Smith in the hope that he would lead the way and take charge. Yorkie, however, seemed intent on a glossy advertisement for bank loans, special terms for saving accounts, and facilities for foreign travel.

Edwards cleared his throat. 'What seems to be the matter?'

'The kids and I aren't going to budge an inch,' said Mrs Lines, 'until they give me some money.'

Other customers either looked round and looked quickly away, or stared stolidly ahead, preferring not to be disturbed by anything so distressingly vulgar.

The bank manager said patiently: 'You don't have any money in your account, Mrs Lines. You can't have what you haven't got.'

'There must be some money in there. Anyway, my husband's monthly pay cheque is due any time.' She swung towards Smith and Edwards. 'Ask these officers.'

Yorkie Smith edged closer to the bank manager. 'Can't we discuss this somewhere . . . well . . . private?'

'I'm not moving,' vowed Mrs Lines, 'until I have some money. For God's sake, I have kids to feed.'

Edwards added his pleas to Yorkie's. 'Can we use your office?'

The bank manager, whose name on a brass plate on the inner door was given as A. L. Hicks, was glad to comply. But
56

Mrs Lines took some shifting. It was only when Edwards began gently shepherding the children towards the door of the inner office, and Hicks and PC Smith edged round behind her like sheepdogs watching for possible divergences, that she allowed herself to be nudged away from the main concourse. As they headed for comparative tranquillity, Yorkie leaned towards Taffy. 'Get hold of Tosh – quickly!'

When the others were out of sight and the door had closed behind them, Taffy moved towards the desk at the end of the counter and nodded towards the phone. The dark-eyed teller smiled permission, and in a subdued tone he broke the news to Viv Martella at her console. Her response was less subdued. Even from this distance he could guess that half of Sun Hill would have heard the news within a matter of seconds. 'Be discreet,' he said lamely. It was a trifle late for that.

Behind Martella, Sergeant Peters whistled a sort of gleeful disapproval through his teeth. 'Get a car along to whisk her out of there sharpish. And I'll see if I can raise Tosh. The fewer we get involved, the better. Don't want us washing our dirty linen in public unless we can help it, do we?'

He went off in search of Lines, and found him in the canteen, looking glum over a cup of coffee. Peters remembered a spell of uproar along the corridor twenty minutes earlier, and sympathised: provoking an argument with Delia, head of the typing pool, was always asking for trouble. Now, unfortunately, he was going to make Tosh even glummer. When he had broken the news, the DC looked incredulous, then swore, then asked Peters for a loan. On that score there was nothing doing. Poor old Tosh had been helped out too many times before: over his father's funeral, over one of the kids' birthdays, and over an advance on a new gas cooker. Life had always been like that for him, and it was high time he found a way of making sure it wasn't like that any longer. Grimly Tosh gave up and headed for the station yard. He swerved his car out of its bay in a wild arc which narrowly avoiding removing the front bumper of Chief Inspector Conway's incoming Jaguar. This was not going to be a good Monday for Tosh.

Martella had succeeded in raising June Ackland on the R/T. 'Could you go to the bank in Townsend Road and meet PC Edwards re a delicate enquiry?'

'Will do.'

As June signed off, Ramsey said: 'Edwards trying to get a mortgage for his rabbit hutch?'

He took a short cut down the narrow chasm of a street plunged in gloom by the high wall of a warehouse, emerged into the main road at the end, and headed back towards the shopping area.

Mr Hicks tapped a few keys, tilted his glasses back on to his forehead, and watched a spread of figures scrolling down the screen before him. Mrs Lines and her kids sat watching: the kids absorbed by the green flicker of the columns, Mrs Lines waiting for the computer to produce the miracle that simply had to happen. Yorkie Smith stood well back against the wall, not wanting to get involved, wishing it was some complete stranger who had been called in to sort out the situation.

The bank manager sat back, sighing. 'There it is, I'm afraid. Your husband drew out £400 on the third and £200 on the fifth. You were then £750 overdrawn.'

A girl came in with a tea-tray. The children's attention was deflected to a plate of biscuits, some of them with pink sugar coatings.

Their mother went on staring at the machine which had so shamefully let her down. 'Why would he draw out so much money?'

Hicks made a non-committal shrug. 'I'm sure you're aware that this is not the first time your account has been overdrawn by such an amount.'

'But it always gets paid back as soon as the pay cheque's come in.'

'Mrs Lines, I've already taken your credit cards from you, but that still hasn't solved the underlying problem. I do have my job to do. As a bank manager I simply can't allow such a state of affairs to continue.'

58

'But I have to live. I have to feed the kids.'

Hicks tipped his spectacles back into place and threw Smith a helpless look, trying to enlist his moral support. Yorkie shifted his weight from one foot to another. 'As soon as we can get hold of Detective Constable Lines he'll be here,' he stalled.

'If you can get hold of him you'll be lucker than me,' said Tosh's wife despairingly.

Not wanting to look again into the wretchedness of her expression, Hicks occupied himself for another couple of minutes with the computer keyboard. The screen flashed no reassurance at him.

Mrs Lines got up and leaned over the desk. 'Couldn't you let me have just twenty pounds to be going on with?'

'Mrs Lines,' said Hicks wearily, 'you and your husband are overdrawn. I have sent numerous letters addressed to both of you. Letters that you have totally ignored.'

It was no use. Yorkie could no longer bear to stand here listening to the humiliation of it all. 'What if I write a cheque for twenty pounds and give it to Mrs Lines?'

'It wouldn't make any difference.'

'I'd lend you the money right this minute,' Yorkie went on to Mrs Lines, 'but I haven't got any cash on . . .'

'I don't want charity.'

There was a dismal silence. At last Hicks reluctantly surrendered. 'All right, Mrs Lines. I will let you draw twenty pounds on the clear understanding that you and your husband make an appointment to come and see me. And by that, I mean together.'

She sniffed and gave a grateful nod.

'Next Tuesday morning. Shall we say half-past nine?'

She nodded again.

'We have simply got to find a way of reducing this overdraft.' The bank manager was determined to rub it in.

Mother and children shuffled towards the door. Yorkie thankfully brought up the rear. The sooner this was over and he was out on the beat again, the better he would be pleased.

'Thank you, Mr Hicks.' Mrs Lines blew her nose. 'I'm sorry for causing such a scene. I feel awful about it, but I was so . . . so desperate.'

He nodded, more anxious to have her off the premises than to offer condolences or any further signs of leniency.

'Next Tuesday morning, then? You'll get Mr Lines to confirm it with me?'

'Yes. Thank you. Yes.'

They emerged by the counter, to find Taffy Edwards on the phone at the far end. Sergeant Peters had called back to say that Tosh was on his way, and there was also a panda car in the offing, coming along in case they needed assistance in removing Mrs Lines and the children.

Edwards glanced at the group leaving the office. 'Looks as if things have calmed down, sarge. Reckon we don't need the panda, but Tosh had better come and collect the pieces. Though' – he lowered his voice – 'I wouldn't want to be in his shoes when his missus gets at him.'

The phone was still in his hand when there was sudden uproar from the main doors. Five men with stockings and black skullcaps over their heads had burst in and fanned out, two with stubby shotguns, one with a large crowbar, and two with automatic pistols.

'Everybody on the floor. Down! Down, the lot of you. Hands on your heads.'

One man, brought up short for a second as he saw the two police officers unexpectedly ahead of him, regained his balance and launched himself at Edwards. A kick into the groin and a wild swipe around the head, and Edwards was doubled up against one of the tables, head down as he gasped agonisingly for breath, with a gun slanting down at him. 'Nobody touch an alarm, or this pig dies.'

Mrs Lines reached out her arms in an attempt to get all three children close to her, hidden by her.

'Stay down. All of you.'

There were thumps and moans of terror as people slumped

to the floor. Yorkie, between Mrs Lines and the counter, tried to edge himself free and make a move. A heavy shoulder crashed into him and rammed him back against a partition. 'You too. You do as you're told.' A pistol was jammed against his head. One of the other men grabbed the bank manager by the arm and twisted it violently. 'Right. Where's the keys?'

The phone which had fallen from Taffy's grasp swung on the end of its cord, silent for an instant and then beginning to chatter plaintively.

'Taff!' Sergeant Peters' voice was only a faint, remote whine beyond the clamour in the banking hall. 'What the hell's going on there?'

Six

Pete Ramsey slowed to negotiate an unusually untidy scatter of parked vehicles along both kerbs of Townsend Road near the London Capital Bank. They surely could not all be the property of people complaining to their bank manager? He edged towards a possible slot, and found himself looking into the cab of a yellow Transit van, its engine still running, with a man in a crash helmet at the wheel.

'Did you see that?'

'Maybe he's collecting his firm's money,' suggested June Ackland.

'Yeah.' Ramsey jarred to a halt and began to get out of the panda. 'And maybe he's in business for himself.'

As he approached the van it juddered forward as if to run him down. Ramsey hammered on the bonnet with his fists. The driver stopped, reversed, and mounted the pavement before shooting suddenly out at an angle and grazing the edge of a parked Cavalier. Ramsey made another hopeless lunge, and heard the belch of a gun and the shattering of bottles in a milk float stationary on the corner of a one-way street. He ducked into the gutter behind the Cavalier, and waved urgently to June to get on the radio, throwing himself to one side as the van roared round in a half-circle as if still seeking to mow him down. Then it was racing off down the street. Ramsey emerged blinking, as if wondering what had blown up in his face.

At Sun Hill Sergeant Peters had turned away from the phone. He was horribly sure that he had interpreted the noises from the bank at the other end of the line correctly.

'Viv. The rest of you. Get all units down to the London

Capital Bank. Tell 'em there are armed men in there. Proceed with caution.'

The urgent messages began to sing out to squad cars at the same time as WPC June Ackland was calling in for urgent assistance. The howls of sirens swept in like a coven of hysterical witches converging on the scene of a bloodletting. They dinned in on Tosh Lines as he turned wretchedly into Townsend Road, to find himself faced by a Transit van belting towards him on the wrong side of the road, and a police car dashing out to give chase. From nowhere another car materialised, and the van driver tried one last burst of acceleration in an attempt to dash between them before the trap closed. He was seconds too late. One car slewed broadside across the road; the other closed in from behind. The officers were out of their seats before the prey could get his door open.

Tosh Lines had been apprehensive and sick inside from the moment he started out from the station. Now he felt ten times worse. He had expected simply to park outside the bank and go in to face whatever unpleasant music there might be waiting for him. Now he could not even get close to the entrance. Two familiar figures flitted across his line of vision. Pete Ramsey and June Ackland were stopping people from crossing the road in front of the bank and waving them urgently away, off the street itself. Tosh parked at an angle which would normally have guaranteed a police swoop and some harsh comments on his interpretation of regulations, yellow lines, and the rest. He was hurrying on foot towards the bank when June spotted him and dashed around a red bus, panting impatiently at the kerb, to intercept him.

'What's happening?'

'Keep back, Tosh. There's a bank raid.'

'You're joking.' He stared at the door and the remarkably empty pavement in front of it. 'Not in that one? My missus and kids are in there.' He tried to push past June and get to the entrance.

'Please! They've got guns.'

'Out of my way.'

He shoved her violently to one side and broke into a trot. Struggling up, she yelled after him, and then saw Ramsey on his way from haranguing the bus driver. 'Pete! Don't let Tosh . . .'

Ramsey saw what was happening, and made a wild dash. He caught up with Lines at the foot of the three steps up to the door. Tosh struggled like a madman, driven on by the one obsession of getting inside and getting close to his wife and kids. June Ackland got up, twisted by the pang of a bruised knee, and tried to totter towards the two men. 'Don't be an idiot,' Ramsey was panting. 'They're armed, you bloody fool.'

'Let me go. Let me . . .'

There was a shotgun blast from a window of the bank. Ramsey was virtually kicked away from Tosh's side as if by a heavy boot in the ribs. He went over backwards and skidded a few feet along the roadway; then curled up, curled in on himself; and then was very, very still.

Lines looked down in disbelief. He made a substantial target, but there was no follow-up shot. June began shouting at him from the cover of the side of the panda, until he stumbled uncomprehendingly towards her and let her pull him down to street level.

'No,' he said. 'No, no.' It became a rhythmic intonation against the background of cars screeching to a halt and the chatter of R/T demands and answers.

Into her radio June said as steadily as she could manage: 'Ramsey has been shot. Repeat. Ramsey's been shot. Urgent assistance needed. Ambulance. And reinforcements.'

Viv Martella was on the air. 'MP from Sierra Oscar. Are there any PT17 officers in the vicinity of Townsend Road? Over.'

In the Chief Superintendent's office a discussion with Christine Frazer of a possible day trip to France for off-duty officers came to an abrupt conclusion as Chief Inspector Conway and Sergeant Peters interrupted. 'We've got a hostage situation, sir. And Ramsey's been shot.'

The machinery spun frantically into motion.

Brownlow summoned Inspector Frazer to his office, checked on deployment of their available forces, and sent out an urgent appeal for armed officers from PT17 to be rushed to the scene. He checked with Peters that an ambulance was already on its way to Ramsey, and that the local hospital had been alerted. Somebody must notify Ramsey's wife. It was Peters who intervened to say that Ramsey wasn't married: he lived with his mother. Then she ought to be picked up and taken to the hospital; and Christine Frazer should be at the hospital too, to report back on Ramsey's condition minute by minute.

'And arrange for Cryer to come in.'

Peters unwisely commented that it was Bob Cryer's day off; but his words trailed away under the Chief Superintendent's withering glare. After an exasperating delay Brownlow got a call through to the Assistant Commissioner to report the situation and announce his decision to get Chief Inspector Conway to the scene as possible negotiator. Maybe it would take time before there was any chance of negotiation, and they would have to sit it out and sweat it out. Brownlow refused to speculate what would happen if the robbers decided to kill some of the hostages and then shoot their way out. Conway had had considerable experience with this tricky kind of situation before ever coming to Sun Hill, and was the best man to take charge on the spot. But while they moved into place and waited, authority was needed for more PT17 men and further officers on standby ready for immediate action of whatever kind proved necessary. The authority was swiftly issued. Pieces were moved expertly into place, according to well established procedures. But theoretical procedures, no matter how meticulously put into practice according to the book, could still not guarantee which way things would go for the hostages. Police procedures, like war games, envisaged a number of rational answers to a variety of difficult situations. What none of them could ever predict would be which way a particular situation would develop, and which answer to prepare for. The Chief Superintendent put the phone down, and told the switchboard to keep his line clear for incoming calls from the scene of operations. Now, here and outside the bank, it was a matter of waiting.

Peters hurried down to the LIO to find Ramsey's home address. Cathy Marshall sprang into action; but then, dismayed, found that for some inexplicable reason her records on Ramsey were incomplete. Certain items in the documentation on his transfer to Sun Hill had been very carefully phrased, and some had been marked strictly confidential on Brownlow's instructions. Those past misdemeanours which had resulted in Ramsey's being shifted from plain clothes back into uniform were not to be allowed to leave a blot on his copybook for ever. Unfortunately, fair as this might be, the careful restructuring of his records had apparently included the elimination of his home address.

'Sorry, sarge.'

'Not your fault, Cathy. Looks as if I'll have to talk to my oppo at Ramsey's last place. Somebody there's bound to know.'

He hesitated in the doorway. Both of them wanted to say something reassuring, but what was there to say? Pete Ramsey, with his cocky manner and sour greenish-brown eyes, had not established himself as one of the most popular members of the team. Partnering him on the beat or in a car, few of the others felt quite at ease. He was prone to cut corners too flagrantly, to swagger and boast too brashly. Occasionally his grudge against the system which, catching up with his card tricks and fiddles and gambling, had demoted him, threatened to boil over into some final damaging showdown. But for all that he had become in his own strutting way one of the Sun Hill bunch. Any one of them might have got in the way of that gun. Injured and maybe dying, he was more a part of the whole essence of the place now than he had ever been before.

'How do you think he's getting on?' Cathy said helplessly.

'God knows. And how are the rest of them getting on out there?' Silently Peters added to himself: *Who's next?*

* * *

Tosh Lines huddled in the shelter of the panda car, his head in his hands, mumbling spasmodically. It was hard to tell whether he was praying or cursing.

'Come on, Tosh, don't take it so hard.' June Ackland tried to comfort him with soothing noises as meaningless as his own. 'You can't blame yourself.'

'I don't know what to do. What to say. I mean . . . oh, God, it was *me*, that's what. If it hadn't been for me . . .' He looked up, and it was plain he could still see vividly the bank ahead of him, and then Pete Ramsey desperately catching up with him, and Ramsey being blasted away from him.

'You weren't to know.'

A distant wailing grew closer, and a shadow fell briefly across the car. An ambulance came to a halt, vulnerably exposed in the middle of the road because there was no space at the kerb. Suddenly there was an eerie stillness. Every man there wanted to be with Ramsey, somehow contributing, helping him on his way. But it was the experienced ambulancemen who gently slid him onto a stretcher and gently slid him into the interior. The doors closed; the ambulance swung tightly round the corner, silently urged on by the watchers.

'God! Please, God, let him be all right.'

The siren clamoured again, distorted and fading between buildings. On the pavement twenty yards away Burnside came to life again and plunged into earnest conference with an armed officer in blue combat gear, directing three men towards the fire escape at the back of the bank. Two marksmen with rifles had already positioned themselves on the rooftop of an insurance company building across the street. Watchful from the kerb below them, but out of the line of direct fire, a control van had its rear doors open. Chief Inspector Conway sat hunched inside beside the radio, in a position almost as despondent as Tosh's, but with his narrow face alert and savage. He looked impatient for some action; but his whole job here was to fight down impatience, restrain wild impulses, not make the area a slaughterhouse – play it

67

cool and be ready for the hard bargaining when it started. Sooner or later that would have to start.

DS Roach positioned two plain clothes officers at the corner round which the ambulance had disappeared. Others were sheltering within an alley to the side of the bank. Whichever way trouble erupted, the exits were all covered now.

One tricky calculation was that of deciding what to do if the gunmen continued to show no signs of coming out and making for those exits.

Conway sat motionless and brooding in the control van, intent on outguessing them. But he had nothing to go on. Nobody had a clue whether the robbers were villains already on the files, whose tactics would follow a familiar pattern, or a completely new team with unpredictable temperaments. A coldly calculating lot, or a group of nut-cases liable to panic and shoot at random? So far all the signs had been that they were dangerously trigger-happy.

The police vehicles were parked in a still, spaced-out battle array. A momentary flicker of movement along a roof parapet four storeys above ceased as two marksmen settled themselves into a posture which turned them into crouching gargoyles, their rifles like juttting water-spouts.

At both ends of the street, cordoned off by the police, curious crowds were gathering. To them it might all have been just a film, something to talk about in the pub or at home that night. Waved back, they eddied about for a while and then trickled back along the pavements, anxious not to miss whatever it was that was going to happen. Burnside watched them angrily from the shelter of a doorway. There would be one hell of an outcry if they got mown down by a burst of firing; and the blame would, as usual, be on the police who were trying to persuade them to go away and at the same time keep an eye on the bank to guard against that very possibility of sudden wild firing.

'Somebody's coming out!'

Conway slid to the road and glared round the rear door of the control van towards the bank entrance. A figure paused

68

in the shadows of the doorway: a figure too dark to be identified for a moment. Rifles high above swivelled round and dipped in a menacing mockery of a salute. Then the dark-clad outline emerged into the daylight.

It was PC Yorkie Smith, without his helmet. He stopped again on the step as if uncertain whether it was safe to come out any further. He appeared to be listening to some command from behind. Then he raised his arms and continued with nerve-racking slowness, hands high above his head. There must be an unseen gunman behind him; and others were following his progress from the rooftops.

Keeping watch on the door of the bank and what might blaze from it without warning, the PT17 officer behind the parapet immediately opposite called down: 'Take it slow. Turn right.'

Like a sleepwalker Yorkie obeyed the instruction and turned right along the pavement.

'Walk down towards the control van.'

Yorkie trod a slow path with hypnotic steadiness. It was impossible to guess whether he had been sent out on a mission, or whether he knew his minutes were numbered – that it was all a trick, a breathing-space into which fire and fury would suddenly be poured, with Yorkie being picked off to distract attention from whatever else the trapped men were planning.

Now he was only a few yards from the control van.

Tosh Lines could restrain himself no longer. In spite of what had happened before and what the result had been for Pete Ramsey, he was flinging himself uncontrollably across the road from the panda car. June made a wild grab but, aching from the last time, was too late.

Burnside swore at the top of his always raucous voice. Rooftop guns veered to one side.

'My missus!' Lines was shouting as he pounded towards Yorkie Smith. He stumbled over the kerb and caught Yorkie's arm. 'My missus . . . the kids . . . are they all right?' He shook the arm madly. 'Are they *all right*?'

69

'Yeah.' Yorkie spoke out of a trance, his eyes glazed. He pulled away from Lines and finally slumped behind the shelter of the control van. 'They're all right,' he said numbly.

But for how long?

Seven

Yorkie Smith sat on the bench in the control van opposite Chief Inspector Conway, trying not to tremble. He had got this far. He was out of it. Yet his lower lip kept betraying him, his fingers would not stay still, his eyes were smarting and he had to tense every muscle to stop himself bursting into tears. This was the end; had to be the end, the bloody end. Weeks ago there had been that hideous couple of hours trying to sort out the traffic mess around the horror of a mother and her child crushed into bloody pulp beneath the swinging cab of an articulated lorry. People panicking, yelling at him, traffic piling up and red-faced drivers yelling while he tried to get an ambulance through the tangle, tried to get help from Sun Hill, tried to calm the public and tried not to look at the blood seeping from the crushed car. All in a day's work, like they said? And now there was a telltale smear of someone else's blood on the road out there, and in his nostrils still the smell of fear suffocating the people inside the bank when they had heard the shooting.

He kept telling himself he was safe, he was out now, they couldn't shove that gun into his teeth any more and couldn't snarl filth at him. But still he had to do what he had been told inside the bank, and then do what he was told here, outside.

He wanted to be sick. But the Chief Inspector was staring at him, indifferent to what human feelings had been like inside that place, intent only on knowing straightforward facts concerning his job.

Never again. Yorkie could never again face going through anything like that fatal accident and now this. But there was no way of making that clear to Conway, right here, right at this moment. Or to Burnside, leaning inquisitively in through the back doors. His own decisions would have to wait. But not for much longer.

Conway said: 'Right, Smith, why did they let you out?'

'Wanted me to tell you, sir, that they were prepared to consider negotiating.'

'Polite of them, I'm sure.'

'On what terms?' growled Burnside.

'They want a phone contact. Want to tell you direct. Say it's up to you to establish contact, and they'll have someone right by the phone. But anyway, they're prepared to talk. Only . . . all talk's off if there's any direct attack on the bank.' Yorkie felt the fear coming back like a sickness scouring the back of his throat. 'Sir . . . who's been shot? Who did they get?'

'Ramsey,' said Burnside. 'Makes it very personal, doesn't it?'

Yorkie put his right hand down to hold on to the side bench and keep his fingers locked there, untrembling.

Conway demanded: 'How many of them in there?'

'Five, sir. I mean, the robbers. There's the hostages, of course – Tosh's wife and kids, and – '

'We're not going to let personal feelings get in our way if we have to move in.'

'No, sir. But I'd say the Lineses were safe. Don't think any harm will come to them.'

'As long as we do what we're told,' observed Burnside.

Conway was reaching for the phone. 'Try to put it out of your mind that an officer and his family are involved.'

'Aren't we forgetting?' Yorkie burst out. Under Conway's basilisk stare he faltered, but remembered Taffy's face and the way he had been doubled up and kicked into a corner by the robbers. 'With respect, sir. PC Edwards has a wife, too.'

'And aren't you forgetting something too, Smith? A lot of those hostages must have families. My concern isn't with individuals, whether they be police officers or not.'

Burnside grunted. There was no way of telling which side

he favoured in the argument. 'Yeah, well. Maybe it'd be a good idea to find out what they want, anyway.'

Conway tensed. This was it. Once he had started on the campaign there could be no turning back: blunders and sidetracks, maybe, but certainly no retreat. He said: 'Right, Smith. I take it they told you which of the bank phones they'd be sitting by?'

Yorkie took a slip of paper from his top uniform pocket, unfolded it, and handed it over. 'That's the number, sir, and they've put the line straight through to the extension on the counter – the one Taffy was using.'

Conway passed the paper to the radio operator tucked well into the inside of the van, and nodded for him to proceed. At the same time he had flicked the switch of the tape recorder, whose reels began to spin. Burnside edged on to the seat beside Conway and reached for a spare earpiece.

There was the crackle of a response from within the bank.

Conway said: 'Chief Inspector Conway here. Are you the one in charge?'

There was a rasped affirmative.

'What do I call you?'

'Names aren't important. And if they were, mine's the last one I'd give you.'

Conway kept his cool. 'Right. What about finishing this business right now? What must be pretty obvious to you is that you're surrounded, that there's never any way you'll get away with the loot, and that – '

'What's obvious,' said the acrid voice, 'and what's important is the fact that we've got twenty-eight hostages. What are you going to do about that?'

'I'd say that it's a matter of what you little lot are going to do about them.' Conway tried to inject a note of sardonic humour into his tone, as if having an argument with a friendly old rival. 'Save a lot of trouble if you sent them out and then followed them with your hands up.'

'You want to talk sense or don't you?'

'All right. What do you suggest?'

'A deal would be in both our interests.'

'Agreed,' said Conway equably. 'What do you have in mind?'

There was a hesitation, then the voice at the other end said: 'So you're beginning to get the picture. That's a start, anyway. Leave it with us, and I'll let you know.'

Conway sat back. Burnside let the earpiece dangle over his shoulder. He looked dissatisfied. There was more than an inkling of somebody trying to manipulate somebody else, trying to fray a few nerves in order to get a promising response before too long. The DI was all in favour of such tactics when he was the one doing the manipulating; less so when he was being left uneasily in the dark at the receiving end.

The commander of the armed contingent paced along the pavement and peered into the van, mutely demanding news. Conway remained stony-faced. Burnside stretched his legs across the cramped interior. Outside, the driver of the stranded bus was leaning out of the far side of his cab, away from the bank's firing line, to argue with a police constable about freedom of movement in a so-called democracy, and the duties of the police in facilitating that movement no matter what other circumstances happened to be preoccupying them. That was not quite the manner in which he expressed himself, but it was a near enough approximation. The constable offered to supervise the evacuation of the bus onto the pavement, shielded from the bank by the bulk of the vehicle itself.

At the radio in the control van, the operator waved at Conway. Another message was coming through. The tape recorder began to rotate again.

'Conway – that was the name, wasn't it?'

'It was. And is.'

'I want a six-seater car with a full tank of petrol, and safe conduct out of here.'

'I'm prepared to consider that.'

'You'd better consider fast. And when you've got it round here where we can see it, I'll release all hostages except the manager.'

A vein beside Conway's forehead pulsed a swollen purple. His lips were sucked deep back into his mouth. He shook his head, though there was no way they could see this at the other end. 'No. I can't allow that.'

'I haven't finished yet. If I see any vehicle tailing me, including helicopters, we'll let him have it.'

'There is no need for any more violence,' said Conway tautly. 'And I cannot allow you to take a civilian hostage. You must know that.'

'My concern is my men. I'll give you fifteen minutes.'

The line went dead.

Conway replaced the receiver and turned back to Smith. 'Are there any other children in the bank besides the Lineses?'

Yorkie could summon up a picture of the whole place: men and women shivering on the floor, the Lines kids clutched close to their mother, two men on guard while the other three ransacked the place, stopping only when it became clear that getting out and through the police cordon unscathed was more important now than merely trying to shift money.

'No, sir. Definitely none.'

Conway glanced at Burnside, who reacted at once. 'No, you can't let that happen.'

'Is Lines still outside – in a car?'

'Yes.'

'It's better he doesn't know.'

'What are you going to do? Go and tell him to take a walk while everybody starts blasting away?'

Painfully Conway made his decision. 'I want a six-seater car ready and waiting.'

'Sir!' exploded Burnside. 'You can't let them dictate to you like this. You're the one who ought to be setting the conditions.'

'I know what I'm doing, Frank. I don't want any more bloodshed.'

Sergeant Bob Cryer strolled along the Parade at a more indolent, easygoing pace than he would have allowed any of

75

his uniformed constables to get away with. Today he was casually dressed in brown jacket and corduroys, with a roll-top sweater knitted by his wife. Decidedly he was not in uniform and not on duty; but he could not help glancing at doorways as he passed, noticing a car with bald tyres and wondering where the beat officer had got to. Unless he and his wife went away for a weekend or a holiday to places quite unfamiliar, there was no way he could kick the habit of noting every little detail. This was his patch. He could have walked along it, round every corner and down every cranny, with his eyes shut. Only that wasn't the way you did the job. He blinked in a sudden shaft of sunlight between two buildings, and wondered ruefully what difference a pair of glasses would make to the way he viewed things. Apart from commenting on a 'floater' in his left eye the optician had sounded reassuring. All the same, there had been a routine cheerfulness in his tone which reminded Cryer of his own manner when promising some anxious woman that her child, or her dog, or her handbag were bound to turn up within the next half-hour.

Away to his right was the slope of Sun Hill, where Alec Peters could well be going through just such a routine right now. Cryer's quickest route lay straight across the junction and on between the market stalls. He had promised to try and remember to pick up a quarter of spiced meat loaf and half a pound of tomatoes on his way home, and the market was as good a place as any. Yet something made him turn right and walk down towards the station. Bob Cryer was not a man with much time for intuition, or psychic forces, or telepathy – it would have brought his career in the Force to a brisk conclusion if some of his superiors had on various occasions been able to read his mind – but like a good doctor he had his hunches, and moments of unease which could not be explained but had to be followed up.

He told himself that he had left a dirty shirt in his locker and wanted to take it home. That was true; but to be honest, the shirt could have waited until tomorrow.

As he crossed the CAD room, Martella at one console was

76

saying, 'The Chief Super's clamouring for me to get hold of Sergeant Cryer,' while at another Alec Peters was pleading for an address from Barton Street station files: 'Trying to get hold of the next of kin of PC Ramsey who was transferred from your station. I believe it's his mum. For some reason our records are incomplete.'

Cryer said: 'Forty-nine Winston Avenue.'

Martella looked round with a gasp of relief. 'Are we glad to see you, sarge.'

'Bob.' Alec Peters rang off and looked equally welcoming.

Cryer stared from one to the other. He could smell real trouble in the air, especially if Brownlow had been sending out messages for him.

'What's all this about?'

Peters said bluntly: 'Ramsey's been shot.'

It was the one word you prayed never to hear. 'Shot.' Cryer made a trembling echo out of it. From the corner of his eye he noticed that Viv Martella was close to tears. At the same time he was instinctively taking his jacket off and getting ready for action. Alec Peters briskly filled him in with the details of the raid so far as they knew them. He waved his arm towards the almost empty offices to either side. Everybody was down at the scene of the action: or, rather, down there waiting for the next burst of action. Brownlow had specifically asked for Cryer to run the office end while Peters had the job of going and breaking the news to Mrs Ramsey. Now that Bob had arrived he could go and do just that. It was not something to look forward to.

As Peters' car pulled away from the yard, Brownlow came downstairs. He was trying to look authoritative, calmly in charge of the situation, but in this lull whose length no one could predict he was too prone to make repeated phone calls to the control van and fussily demand information as to who was where and whether further armed reinforcements had arrived. Three times he assured Cryer of the complete confidence he had in Conway's skills as a negotiator. There had been that brilliant cooling-down he had managed at the Indian takeaway siege. And the long-drawn-out confrontation with the pickets threatening to drag out a printing works manager barricaded in his office.

And, Cryer added wryly to himself, that incredible cock-up over the two freaks loose in a primary school.

Cryer's opinion of the chief inspector contained many reservations. Even in smaller crises Conway was too prone to lose his cool and thrash about in several directions at once. In a big one like this, there was no telling if or when he would let fly.

'Great confidence in Paul,' Brownlow repeated. 'So has the Commissioner.'

Martella answered a call, and slewed round on her chair. 'Sergeant Peters is with Mrs Ramsey. She doesn't feel she can face going to the hospital. He's going to stay with her a while in case she changes her mind.'

'Inspector Frazer's at the hospital. She ought to have rung in by now. See if you can raise her and find if there's any news.'

The news was that Ramsey was in the operating theatre undergoing emergency surgery. Nobody would say anything. Christine Frazer sounded very depressed.

'Now let me have another word with Mr Conway.'

As Brownlow talked, a light green Ford Granada arrived under the window. Two men in brown overalls got out without fuss and came quietly into the station. They waited, apparently quite relaxed, until Brownlow had finished his conversation, and then explained what they proposed for the van. It was risky. The moment the robbers suspected a trick, there was no telling what they might be capable of doing in revenge. But someone had to make a move.

And somebody had to drive the van to the bank and stay very calm while setting the whole thing up. Again, no way of predicting the immediate outcome: no telling whether they would add the driver to their group of hostages or find some other way of dealing with him.

Cryer said: 'I'll do it.'

78

'No,' said Brownlow. 'I want you here, Bob. That's why I sent for you.'

'There isn't anyone else.' As Brownlow looked uncertain, Cryer went on doggedly: 'This one's mine, guv. If it isn't done properly . . . well, it's down to me.'

He went out into the yard. One of the men in overalls opened the driver's door for him and went round to lean over from the other side. He reached across Cryer's knee to show him a blue wire tucked neatly under the dashboard near the ignition switch. When the car stopped outside the bank, he must reach for the wire before anyone had a chance of noticing what he was doing, give it a little tug, and then push the end back out of sight. Bob Cryer experimented two or three times with his little finger to make sure it could be managed unobtrusively, then nodded and settled himself behind the wheel.

'Right.' The electrician backed off and slammed his door. 'All yours, mate.'

Cryer drove off along familiar streets, slowing at a junction as crowded as it always was on weekdays, and wondered if he would ever see it again. It was all so ordinary and everyday; but what was waiting for him outside that bank was far from ordinary and everyday.

There was no point in believing the worst before it happened. The only thing to do was to drive carefully, and get there.

Cheif Inspector Conway rubbed a hand wearily across his face and looked at his watch. If they didn't ring, if they had just been buying time while they devised something inside that building . . .

The phone rang.

'Do you have a car ready?'

'One's on its way. But I can't allow you to take any hostages.'

'You don't expect me to believe you'll let me and my men drive away, just like that?'

79

'I would prefer you to give yourself up,' said Conway stonily. 'I must remind you that you're surrounded by armed police, and that if anyone's life is endangered . . .' He and Burnside, on the extension, exchanged glances. Both of them were aware of the unresponsive stillness. 'Are you still there?' It was no time to betray panic or uncertainty. 'Are you there?'

'This is my final word. I want the car outside the entrance in five minutes. I'll release all the hostages. Except for the copper.'

'I'm sorry, but I can't – '

'A gun will be pointed at his head the whole time. Understood?'

'But . . .'

'The time for talking is over.'

A receiver was replaced. Conway hung up his own phone and turned to Burnside. 'Have the car placed outside the bank door, facing this way.'

'You can't do that. You can't let them go! They can pick up as many hostages as they need,' raged Burnside, 'between here and wherever they're going.'

'Don't argue. Do it.'

Burnside slid resentfully out and edged round onto the pavement.

The Granada came into view and pulled up behind the control van. Dourly Burnside obeyed orders, biting off each word as he said it, pointing Bob Cryer over in the direction of the bank. Cryer reversed into the lane beside it, followed every inch of the way by the rooftop marksmen, and then edged out to park as instructed at the foot of the shallow steps from the entrance.

In spite of all the men and vehicles in the street, a hush hung over the whole scene.

From the far side of the road Yorkie Smith could see Cryer getting out of the car and walking steadily away, almost along the path Yorkie himself had taken. He knew what it felt like; could almost feel himself pacing it out again, and felt his stomach contract. Every muscle in his body ached in tune with the sergeant's. Or was Sergeant Cryer now hardened to that kind of thing? It was impossible to believe that anyone could ever be that hardened.

There was a flurry of movement in the bank entrance. People began blundering out of the doors and down towards the car, slowly at first and then in a turbulent wave.

'What the hell are they doing?' Conway demanded.

'Targets are among the hostages,' said a voice over the R/T from one of the armed officers.

Burnside got the message. 'They're using the hostages as cover, that's what they're bloody well doing.'

The robbers were driving the flinching men and women into a protective circle around the Granada. One of the masked men held his gun jammed into a bank clerk's back, prodding him forward to load some dustbin bags into the boot. They had no intention of leaving completely empty-handed.

When the boot lid was slammed down, the five moved fast. The doors of the car were flung back, one man was sliding into the driver's seat, another thrust PC Edwards into the back seat, and then they were all in and the hostages were scattering wildly. The driver reached for the ignition key and turned it.

Nothing happened.

'Go! Get going!'

'It won't start.'

'Don't be bloody stupid. It got here, didn't it?'

'It's a trap.'

A gun was pressed against Edwards' head. 'You get in there and drive.'

The driver flipped his door open and got out. Two from the back seat forced Edwards out and along the side of the car. The shield of hostages had thinned as they ran in all directions, diving behind police vehicles and round the back of the stationary bus. Tosh Lines swept the smallest of his children up into his arms, while his wife and the others clawed at him, sobbing. But the gun jabbing against Edwards' head was a warning to anyone who risked opening fire from the rooftops or the shelter of the alley opposite. The targets might be clearly exposed now; but so was Taffy. Urged along the side of the car, he lurched towards the driver's open door.

Every eye watched him; watched him duck his head to get in; and then saw him suddenly crouch and straighten up again. Without warning he flailed out with a wild punch, crashing the man with the gun into the door and then throwing his whole weight around it.

Yorkie Smith's heart began to pound. Couldn't be anything like Taffy's, though – Taffy running madly across the road, arms pumping, too desperate even to try and weave an erratic path. Any minute now there would a burst of firing, and more blood spurting on to the road, and another victim to keep Pete Ramsey company.

The firing, when it came, was a screaming fusillade from the rooftops. One man spun round and collapsed against the offside front wheel of the Granada. Two tried running, as madly as Taffy Edwards had done, one wildly raising his shotgun only to be cut down.

Edwards reached the front of the control van, fell face down on its bonnet, and would have crumpled to the pavement if Burnside had not been there to catch him.

'It's all right, Taff, it's over. It's over, son.'

Yorkie Smith could no longer control his near-epileptic shivering. For him, too, it was over. Very definitely over. The accident, and now this . . . he had had enough. There was nothing he could do about it until they had prepared the official report on this, and he had added his own details to the rest. Then would be the time to make some decisions of his own and put all this behind him.

He forced himself to walk shakily towards Taffy Edwards and give the DI a hand in propping him upright.

Enough was enough.

Eight

Carol Braithwaite had been at the back of Yorkie Smith's mind during the years he had been away in London. Occasionally she came into sharp focus again, especially after seeing her when he visited his parents in Brankley – once in the distance, once crossing the street to the newsagent's. Nothing much changed in Brankley apart from the takeover of a small grocery shop by a chain too small to call its premises supermarkets, the switches in petrol company signs as the garage changed hands from time to time, and the appearance on a ridge five miles to the east of a Sheffield housing overflow. Carol had not changed much, either, when he saw her in those passing moments. This time it was different, as they came face to face in the street.

'Hello, Tony. A bit far off your beat, aren't you?'

One good thing about getting back home was that people called him Tony. He was so used to being called Yorkie that it took an hour or two to adjust whenever he came back, but it was nice. It made him a person again instead of just a stock character, a Jock or a Taffy or Paddy or Yorkie.

'Serious investigation,' he said archly.

It was true, in a way, but he wasn't going to let on just what kind of investigation. Not that she would be particularly interested, he supposed. It was a long time since they had gone up on the fells together, and talked a load of rubbish, and had those fumbling, blundering but marvellous spells together without anyone ever suspecting. Or maybe a few suspicions had floated about a bit. Her father and mother had shown signs of expecting something to come of it, the way they knocked about together. Mr Braithwaite's handshake and good wishes when young Smith went off to join the Met had been a lot less than cordial.

Automatically he looked across the low wall of the brook to where the fields began to rise to the rougher moors, criss-crossed with drystone walls and restless with a hoarse breeze which never quite stopped. It caught him in the guts, worse than any kick in the guts from any villain on the manor. He realised that Carol had turned her head and was looking reminiscently in the same direction. A faint flush tinged her cheeks.

'Must be a bit tame here, after London.'

'I wouldn't mind something a bit tamer.'

'Rough, is it? But really exciting, I bet.'

He had half forgotten what a slow, inviting sort of voice she had, always tinged with a hint of laughter – not laughing at people, but enjoying being with them and sharing a smile. She was a great one for sharing. He wondered who she was sharing her life with right now. She was smartly dressed, smarter than what he had been used to in the village even a few years ago, and slimmer than when their main treats had been the food and booze at the weekly disco or a night out in Sheffield. Probably married to some upwardly mobile young wheeler-dealer there, though she was still walking about the village during a weekday lunchtime: maybe living in one of the commuters' tarted-up cottages along the bank of the stream, and shopping for the whiz-kid's supper.

Carol stroked a tendril of corn-gold hair across her forehead with long, slender fingers. She was not wearing a wedding ring. Not that that meant a lot nowadays. Her eyes were blue and still shy, as he remembered them; shy and yet smiling, waiting trustingly to be made happy rather than hurt.

She said: 'Here for long?'

'The rest of the week.'

'Oh. Holidays, then? Or are you on a secret assignment to find a mysterious dead body up on Brankmoor?'

'I remember one body up on the moor,' Tony Smith blurted out suddenly. 'Only it wasn't dead. Not dead at all.'

The pinkness flooded entrancingly up from the swell of her breasts and around her throat, to meet the flush in her cheeks. He was amazed at his own words and the way they had come out. Now he had no idea what else to say. Nor had Carol. They stood there outside the Post Office while a few locals went in and came out, glancing speculatively at them. It would be all over the village in no time. Yet there wasn't anything to spread over the village; not really anything to talk about. Certainly Tony Smith and Carol Braithwaite were not talking.

'Well.' She looked up at the Diamond Jubilee clock. 'I'd better get a move on, or they'll be shut.'

'Yes.'

'If you're here for a week, perhaps I'll see you around.'

'Yes.' With an awful feeling that if she walked away down the street he might somehow not bump into her again during the whole of the rest of the week, he said: 'It's super weather, just like I remember it. I haven't had a chance of walking round the old places for ages. Might have forgotten the way.'

Every little smile of hers, every gesture, even when she fumbled with the clasp of her handbag for want of something better to do, added growing vividness to his hazy memories of her. How the hell could they ever have faded away into such a haze? She was so real.

'I'm working in the estate agent's down the street,' said Carol.

'I wasn't actually thinking of buying any property. Not right away, anyway.'

'We shut Wednesday afternoons.'

On Wednesday they walked up to the Warlock Stone and paced round it as every kid in the neighbourhood had done a hundred times. Even now he doubted if he could accept a dare to go round it widdershins. Fortunately, Carol did not suggest it. He told her that he had had enough of policing in London, couldn't breathe the air down there any longer, and his stomach wouldn't stand it any longer. He waited for her expression to change. She would never call him a coward

85

outright, it wasn't her way. But she would think it and somehow show it. Leaving Brankley in a fine swagger, and coming back with his tail between his legs: that was the picture, wasn't it?

Carol's smile faded, and her eyes clouded with the terror of what he was telling her. Instinctively she grabbed his hand and held it tight. Her clasp was firmer, less unsure and vaguely sentimental than it had been those years ago; yet reassuring rather than demanding.

On the Friday afternoon he was invited to tea with the Braithwaites. He hesitated, not wanting to be rushed, yet in one way wanting just that – to have his mind made up for him, to be rushed out of the mire into the free northern air. Mr Braithwaite asked him bluntly about his job, and even more bluntly asked just how scared he had had to be in order to chuck up a career like that. It was good to be just as forthright back. Up here there were no station politics and no first-name stuff one minute, *constable* and *sir* the next, when it suited them rather than suited you. Mr Braithwaite said what he thought. Tony Smith replied with exactly what he thought, take it or leave it.

By the end of the meal Mr Braithwaite was offering to take it. There was a vacancy for a strong, honest young man, especially one with police experience and driving experience, in his Peak Security organisation. There could be rough patches here, just as in London. If there was perfect honesty everywhere and no vice and no crime in the country, nobody would need security firms and armour-plated vans. But at least there were fewer full-time hoodlums and a lot less bloodshed over the lonely moors and dales, or even in the streets of Sheffield, than in the wildernesses around Sun Hill. What you could rely on was more pay and regular hours. The company's main business was in swift and safe transport of fragile specialised goods and urgent packages rather than cash. 'Not the sort of thing even our most ambitious local villains would know how to handle.' And anyway, if you had to take a few risks in life, wasn't it better to take them where the air was cleaner and the landscape lovelier and the whole cost of living a lot less than in the southern rat race?

It was all too neat. It could all be a kind of trap: Carol listening gravely, pretending not to smile and pretending not to care whether he came back and settled down here, and Mr Braithwaite pretending to talk purely business, and Mrs Braithwaite making a fuss over tea and biscuits and a dozen things which had nothing to do with what they were talking about. A cosy, comfortable trap.

There was nothing terribly wrong about being comfortable.

He looked at Carol, who resolutely looked away as if honestly not wanting to influence him or offer anything on her own account. Mr Braithwaite never as much as hinted that his daughter went with the job.

It was such a short time ago that Tony Smith had said he was not actually thinking of buying any property in this neighbourhood.

On his way back in the train he looked out of the window and recalled the same scenery reeling away behind him as he set out full of high hopes, on his way to London where everyone wanted to go. The lads in the village had been full of envy. There had been adventure in the air. Yorkshire was behind him, other counties of no importance were sliding away as he watched. He was going to be a tough policeman, was going to win awards and decorations, promotion to high rank, and become the terror of villains and scourge of petty swindlers. London would be well and truly cleansed by the time he had finished with it.

Now there was going to be a quite different finish. Or a new beginning. The closer he got to London, the easier he could anticipate the cracks they would all be making at Sun Hill once they heard the news: going back to the sticks, playing the local big-shot, marriage to the boss's daughter as part of the deal. So let them make a big thing of it. It would soon be over and he would be on his way back north. London was not a place of adventure any more, but violence out of all control. It was dirty, and bad for your health.

All right, he was opting out. Maybe they wouldn't say it out loud, but they would remember the way he reeled under shock, and mutter about cold feet, a yellow streak, and all the rest of it. He had to face up to that. Sure, he was walking out before his feet got too cold to keep him upright. Sure, somebody had to try and cope, to keep the crime-sodden city's corruption within bounds; and here he was walking out on it. But he was going to be honest about it.

As he took the Tube back to his digs, he could feel himself becoming Yorkie Smith again. But only for a little while now. Soon he would be Tony Smith once and for all.

One week after Yorkie handed in his resignation, news came that Pete Ramsey was pulling round and out of danger. A few days later it was officially confirmed that he was to be invalided out of the Force, and there was speculation about the kind of pension he would be getting. It was one way of leaving the Force. Yorkie was content to leave without any such pension. Back in London, the old horrors were stirring again. He couldn't wait, now, to leave the place far behind him. Everything had gone sour. He did not want to be shot dead, did not want to be savagely wounded, for all the disability pensions in the world.

On his final day he reported for duty as usual, and was in the locker room changing ten minutes before 6.00 a.m. parade. Only this time he was not pushing oddments on to the shelf, but clearing bits and pieces out. He held up a clutch of magazines which had accumulated at the back of the locker. 'Anyone want these?'

'Got any *Beanos*?' asked Melvin.

Reg Hollis, unable to resist the slightest chance of anything going for free, put his head round the metal door. 'What are they?' He was disappointed by the sight of the old issues of a sports monthly and some earnest police handouts. 'Read all those.' He shied violently away from a charity leaflet appeal from the RNLI which fell out from between the pages of a glossy coloured catalogue. 'Anything else?'

'Claire Brind's got first option on his jockstrap,' contributed Tony Stamp.

Yorkie turned and offered two squash balls to Hollis, who eyed them dubiously. 'Not perished, are they?'

Something that had been overlooked for some time now lay flat at the back of the shelf, where Yorkie must have buried it beneath spare socks, Coke cans and odd papers. He took it out and folded back one curling edge. It was a photograph of his passing-out day at Hendon. If he had not known exactly where he appeared in the line-up, he would have had difficulty in distinguishing his own face from all the other smiling, terribly eager faces. He wondered what had happened to all the rest of them: how many had started clawing their way up the ladder, and how many had packed up at one stage or another, just as he was doing today?

Somehow he was reluctant to leave the locker room and follow the others as they jostled out. It was nothing to get sentimental about. His last parade was just coming up, and he was glad about that and not sorry about it, not by any means. Yet he was the last in the locker room, glancing aimlessly around, as Sergeant Peters put his head round the door.

'Just eight hours to freedom, then?'

'That's it, sarge.'

'We'll miss you.' Peters, too, was looking round the room, but more purposefully than Yorkie. 'Er . . . will you be taking your snooker cue?'

Yorkie decided it was time to head for parade in the ILO room.

It all seemed brighter and more immediate than usual. It was impossible to believe he would not be here tomorrow or any other morning, listening to Sergeant Cryer's dry, matter-of-fact voice running through the schedule for the day. It was all at once as fascinating and action-packed as the day when he first nervously showed up on parade, trying to memorise every last little detail so that he could go out and deal unerringly with every bit of trouble that raised its head.

'Problems expected in the rush hour, junction of Gilfillan Road and Robey Street, due to roadworks for cable TV. WPC Brind to attend for point duty, please.' Claire Brind's pert, outgoing little face made it clear that Bob Cryer had already blighted her day and that from now on her thoughts would be ingoing and none too savoury at that. 'Come on, Claire' – Cryer had not apparently been looking at her, but missed nothing – 'you know you love that sort of thing. And when it's slackened off, on to five beat after breakfast. Hollis, three beat for you. And could you call at Lombardy House on the Pilbeam Estate. The odd couple at number twenty were spring cleaning in the night and woke the neighbours. Just make sure everybody's happy, will you?'

Reg Hollis groaned. Groaning was something he had a talent for.

Inspector Christine Frazer slipped unobtrusively into the room as Cryer continued: 'Malcolm, four beat. Ken front desk, Taffy six beat, and George in panda eighty-five. And that brings us to Yorkie Smith, who in the time-honoured tradition of the service will be spending his last day on the job scrounging about inside with a bit of paper in his hand. Right, any questions?'

'Yes,' said Tony Stamp. 'What time's the booze-up?'

It was left to Yorkie to provide the most important information of the day. 'Two o'clock onwards in the *Grapes*.'

'And I'm sure,' Frazer intervened, 'that I can depend on you all to behave in a manner the Commissioner would expect.'

Cryer whistled thoughtfully, and nodded. 'I'll order the ambulance and TSG for midnight.'

As parade finished and they all began to disperse, Hollis turned plaintively to Yorkie Smith, the only one today willing to provide an audience. 'I've always said Cryer had his favourites. Ever since I came off the ILO's job he's had it in for me. All gutty duties, never the sniff of a motor.' As Yorkie began to saunter away he followed him. 'You're the one who ought to be doing this Lombardy House thing.'

90

'Your beat now, Reg.'

'Not till tomorrow, by rights,' Hollis whined. 'And you're on their wavelength.'

'Time you started tuning in, then, isn't it?'

As Hollis moved reluctantly across the CAD room to the corridor, Sergeant Peters lifted his gaze from his console. 'You on three beat, Reg? Then this one's for you.' He jerked his thumb at the screen. 'Kilby Street. Intruders reported in video shop next to laundrette.'

Hollis's dark, dissatisfied face lit up with the prospect of confusing things by a genuine complaint. 'Yes, but sarge, I can't be in two places at once, can I? I'm supposed to be going to Lombardy House.'

Yorkie said: 'I'll go.'

'Lombardy House?' said Hollis hopefully.

'No. Kilby Street.'

It was a street with an unhealthily large number of shops boarded up on one side, facing a row on the other side which were attempting a comeback, some of them newly painted, some empty but far from derelict. The video shop still had some faded lettering above the window, and posters within the window, backed by the thick lattice of a security grill. Peering into the gloomy interior in the pallid morning light, Yorkie could make out very little other than a blurred reflection of his panda car behind him. Certainly there could be precious little worth breaking in for. He reached for his radio.

'Sierra Oscar from 148, receiving? Over.'

'Receiving, 148,' said Sergeant Peters. 'Over.'

'This video shop, sarge. Do we have an owner?'

'Latest keyholder we have is a Mr Cooper. No answer on his home number.'

'Who's the informant?'

'Mr Shah, owner of the laundrette.'

Yorkie moved a few paces along the pavement. The door was open and two dim lights were on, but there was nobody in attendance on the machines.

'He's not around.'

'Well, he wouldn't be, would he? He's got another twenty to open for business.'

Yorkie went back to the video shop and tried the door again. It was locked with a Yale lock as well as a mortice. He paced round the back, along a damp-smelling entry, and found no sign of forced entry at the rear door. It was difficult to imagine what could have led anyone to report intruders.

'All right,' Peters was saying. 'Book it and leave it, then.'

Yorkie leaned against the car and wrote a brief report in his pocket-book. He was snapping it shut and preparing to get into the car when he was aware of a shifting of faint shapes beyond the blur of the lattice. As he took a step back across the pavement, there was the rattle of locks turning, and the door opened. A blonde woman in her thirties stood in the doorway. She was wearing a dark green coat with luridly orange trimmings, and her makeup was just a bit over the top for this time of the morning. Her attitude was cocky and the lines cutting into the corners of her very red mouth made it look as if that mouth could get loud and argumentative without a lot of provocation; but at the moment she seemed friendly enough – admiring, even.

'That was quick. We haven't even rung yet.'

She held the door open. Yorkie walked in warily. There was not much more to see once he was inside than there had been through the window. One large cardboard box stood on a dusty counter at the back of the shop, overlooked by a stack of empty shelves. Racks along the side walls were just as empty except for a couple of buckled video covers sporting a monster with bared fangs and a raven-haired girl with a largely bared bosom.

As the woman closed the door behind him, Yorkie said: 'Can you tell me what you're doing on these premises, madam?'

'Sorry if you've been knocking' – her voice had a piercing Cockney rasp – 'but we've been exploring upstairs.' Before Yorkie could ask, a man appeared from a door behind the counter, brushing dust from his shoulders. 'Sherry Broome,' said the woman. 'And this is my husband Mick. We're the new tenants.'

Mick nodded deferentially. He was taller than his wife, but stooped as if waiting for something to clobber him from behind. It was obvious which one of them was the power behind the partnership.

'You mean,' said Yorkie, 'this is your shop?'

'As of this morning, yes.'

'And would you have any identification, love – proof of ownership?'

'The paperwork's in the pipeline. We've got the keys, of course.'

The two of them and the bunch of keys she was holding out looked convincing enough, but Yorkie felt a tingle of unease about the whole set-up. 'Six o'clock's a funny time to open, isn't it?'

'We're not open. We're just here. Couldn't sleep. It's our first business, see. Mick used to be a bus driver, didn't you, Mick?'

'Yuh.' Mick Broome seemed to be making a sad confession rather than merely confirming what his wife had said.

'Only we thought we were taking over lock, stock and barrel.' Sherry Broome waved a hand around the empty interior, and her cockiness faded. 'It's all gone. That's why we were just going to ring you.' She tried a wan smile. 'It's a bit worrying, really.'

Yorkie was about to suggest that they all sat down and went through the details, only there was nowhere to sit, until Mick Broome went through to the back and found a rickety old kitchen chair. Yorkie waved Mrs Broome into it, while he and Broome leaned against the counter.

'Now, when were you last here?'

'Last Wednesday.'

And the shop, Sherry Broome confirmed with bewilderment and mounting indignation, had been fully stocked then. It had all been part of the deal. The draft lease, which was of course in the pipeline as she had said, covered everything like

93

that. They had paid their deposit, and Mrs Durban and her husband had handed over the keys and been very friendly and helpful. It had been agreed that the Broomes could move in today. There was so little fuss: this being their first business venture, they were amazed at how simple it all was, and how decent the Durbans had been. They had stuck to the deposit given in their newspaper advert, not trying to put it up once they knew the Broomes were serious.

Beginning to sense the worst, Yorkie said: 'And how much did you actually pay, if you don't mind my asking?'

'Show him the advert, Mick.'

Mick Broome fished a folder out of the cardboard box and handed over a cutting to Yorkie. He made a quick estimate in his head. The lease offered was at £120 a week, two months' deposit to be paid in advance. So they must have put down something in the region of £1,000.

'On the basis of their takings so far this year,' Sherry Broome hastened to explain, worried by the look in Yorkie's eye, 'we'll easily . . .'

'Cash?' said Yorkie.

'Oh, yeh. They preferred cash as a sign of good faith, didn't they, Mick?'

As Mick Broome summoned up a gloomy nod, a key turned in the Yale lock of the front door. An Asian couple in their early twenties came in smiling; and stopped smiling when they saw that there were already people on the premises.

Yorkie said: 'Can I help you, sir?'

The young man slowly crossed the floor. 'I don't think so. Why are you in our shop?'

'*Your* shop?'

'Yes. We are the new tenants.'

Nine

Reg Hollis plodded without enthusiasm into the complex of buildings, trodden earth, skimpy grass, and concrete-slab courtyards which made up one of the council estates high on the list of Sun Hill troubles. This area was not as violent as two of the others, but managed to provide an unreasonable proportion of day-to-day irritation. He approached the high-rise block to the west with some trepidation, and before tackling the lift or the stairs decided to do a cautious recce. Any hint of aggro, and he wanted a clear escape route and time to call for assistance.

Between the billowing sheets on a washing line he found himself confronting a cheerful sixty-year-old woman with three plastic clothes-pegs between her teeth. She summoned up the best smile she could manage without losing the pegs, and kept him waiting while she spread another sheet along the line. One corner of it slapped damply into Hollis's face.

'Good morning – Mrs Flowers, isn't it?' He tried to make sure she knew her place, having heard about her from Sergeant Cryer as a helpful person on the estate, and wanting to make sure that she helped him on his terms and not on her own. 'Don't think we've met. Reg Hollis, Sun Hill.'

'You're the new one, are you?' She was plump and sure of herself and of most other things. 'He said there'd be a new one.'

'He . . .?'

'Shame he's leaving. We were very fond of our Yorkie.'

'Yes, well. London's got too much for him. Y'know, life at the sharp end. Off to bury himself in Yorkshire.'

'What's wrong with Yorkshire? You ever been there, young man?'

'I've been past it,' said Hollis damningly.

'Pass me them knickers.'

There was a basket of damp washing at his feet. Without realising what he was doing, he stooped and picked up a pair of puce knickers and then, trying to reassert himself, said brusquely: 'About last night. Flat twenty. All quiet now, is it?'

'Just about. High time, too. I kept ringing the council, but there's never anybody there. Not awake even now, if you ask me, while there's some of us could really be doing with some shut-eye.'

'Nobody hurt?'

'Only 'cos nobody was walking underneath. I mean, fair's fair. I'm all for live and let live, but if he's gonna make a habit of heaving tables off balconies . . .' She stuffed another cluster of pegs in between her teeth and moved methodically along the line, hooking the clothes basket towards her with a practised turn of the right foot.

It began to dawn on Reg Hollis what Sergeant Cryer had meant when referring airily to a matter of spring cleaning.

'Are they . . . uh . . . in now, d'you know?'

'Raymond's upstairs. Pauline's round the front.' Renee Flowers waved a free hand towards the corner of the block. 'Round the front.'

Hollis tried a sociable smile, but was not very good at it. He was halfway towards the path leading to the front of the building when it struck him that he was still holding the knickers. Making a flourish of passing them gallantly across the line, he made a hasty escape.

On the thin coating of grass below the towering façade of flats was a kitchen table of steel and plastic. Alongside it was a matching chair, occupied by a forty-year-old woman with a strained yet philosophical expression. She had scrawny legs, pale but for one prominent varicose vein, and her slippers looked too flimsy to be resting on the dewy grass. What might have been a housecoat or a dressing gown was wrapped round her body. She was eating one end of a loaf torn in half, smeared with margarine, and drinking from a carton of milk. Beyond the far side of the table lay two more chairs, a pedal bin, and a small cupboard with doors of shattered glass hanging loose.

Hollis glanced apprehensively at the balcony immediately above. Nobody seemed to be stirring. He drew himself up to his full height, but chose the side of the table farthest away from the immediate line of descent.

'Mrs Kellow?'

'Sit down. Bad manners to stand when people are eating.' As Hollis obediently groped for a chair and set it upright, she jerked her head towards the heavens. 'He's all right now. He's had his pills.'

'Oh. Good. Yeh, fine.'

'The way the folk downstairs were carrying on, we thought your mates in the flat hats would be along to cart him off any minute. But they know he's as good as gold when he's had his pills. Don't suppose they'd want him in their nice flash car anyway.'

'No, I suppose not.'

It was all a bit weird, sitting out here with this slack-shouldered woman while a few men off to work gazed curiously at them. Somewhere a radio started rattling out some morning news, a weather forecast, and traffic warnings. Quiet, though, just sitting here.

Pauline Kellow made an abrupt movement. For a second Hollis had the alarming impression that she was pushing a half-gnawed chunk of bread towards him in an invitation to share her breakfast. But she had put her head back and, without warning, was bellowing at the first-floor window immediately above.

'Wake up, you! I'm not lugging this stuff back upstairs on me own, y'know. You threw it, you take it back.'

Hollis had another stab at taking charge of the situation. 'Why did he throw it out in the first place?'

'Because it was dirty.' She stood up, swept crumbs and the

milk carton off the table across the grass, and said: 'Well, come on. You can give us a hand if he won't.' She got her arms round the cupboard and began tottering to the stairs at the end of the block. 'Bring the table, will ya.'

Hollis stared after her. He was tempted to make a dash for the nearest street and leave her to it. But he found himself picking up the table and following.

'Hey!' There was a roar from above. Raymond Kellow was leaning out of an open window. He was large and unkempt, with braces twisted over fat shoulders, and his expression was as murky as his vest. 'That's my table.'

'Shut up, you stupid fool,' his wife cried back.

'That's mine.'

Raymond disappeared from the window, and Pauline said blandly to Hollis: 'He thinks you're nicking it, you see. Stupid bloody fool.'

The sooner the table was on the landing and off his hands, the safer Hollis would feel. He panted up the first few steps behind Pauline, just as her husband came into view at the top of the flight. He had no socks on, and his shoes were slopping unlaced around his ankles.

'My table . . .'

His right arm was raised. Reaching the landing, Pauline knocked it back to his side. 'Don't you touch him. He's helping. Because you're too lazy.'

'I'm not lazy.'

'Well, go and get the chairs then.' She might have been talking to a pettish child. 'You hear me? Get them chairs.'

'I thought we were going shopping.' He sounded immediately humbled.

'It's too early.'

'Why?'

She shoved him to one side. 'Go and get the chairs.'

Raymond edged meekly past Hollis and went downstairs. At ground level he veered towards the end of the washing line, until jolted away by another screech from Pauline on the balcony.

Hollis, dumping the table outside the open door of their flat, watched with a mixture of fascination and creeping contempt until his radio sputtered into life. It was Sergeant Peters asking how he was getting on. Hollis reported exactly how he was getting on, and exactly what he thought of this kind of waste of police time, and the report he would submit to the next Federation enquiry, and why he was quitting the scene this very minute.

The Kellows seemed calm enough and were carrying a few remaining pieces back upstairs in a companionable silence as he took the path round the corner.

Heading off with her empty washing basket, Renee Flowers looked back over her shoulder. 'Raymond used to do whatever Yorkie told him,' she confided wistfully.

Yorkie Smith's radio report to Sun Hill was a remarkable catalogue of disasters. Within the space of forty minutes he had collected in the confines of the video shop no fewer than fourteen people. The Shavastras had arrived soon after the Broomes, and at regular intervals there came three other couples and two distraught, willowy men. They had a lot in common: all their tempers were frayed, all their hopes had been dashed, and each couple had lost a thousand quid. They all had sets of keys, and they had all assumed they would be moving in this morning and getting down to business without delay. This turmoil was not the atmosphere in which Yorkie had visualised spending his last few leisurely hours in the region of Sun Hill.

When the door opened yet again he felt a pang of despair, fully expecting another deluded couple armed with duplicate keys, adding their voices to the chorus of accusation. Instead it was DS Ted Roach, for once in history a welcome sight.

Roach slapped Yorkie on the arm. 'Peters and Cryer filled me in on this. Told me there wouldn't be any booze-up this afternoon if I didn't dig you out. So push off back to the nick and get yourself some breakfast.'

'Thanks a lot, sarge. But if you want me to stand by – '

'On your way. You'll need a solid foundation for the liquid intake. Oh, and Conway wants a word with you when you get back.'

Yorkie was not going to argue any further, especially as he had just noticed another middle-aged couple approaching the shop and looking possessively at the posters in the window. He drove thankfully back to Sun Hill.

Chief Inspector Conway was crossing the custody area as he arrived, and waved towards his office. Yorkie followed him in.

'Ted Roach got the video shop under control?'

'They keep rolling in, sir.'

'More of them? Stroll on! Would *you* hand over a thousand quid for a set of keys and nothing in writing?'

'No, sir. But then I'm not a Londoner.'

Conway sat in the chair behind his desk and smiled thinly. 'No.' Unexpectedly he added: 'Which is a pity.' Somehow it made Yorkie feel sheepish and guilty. 'Anyway, the Chief Super'll be making all these official noises when he sees you. Unofficially I thought I'd just like to say good luck for the future. But I can't pretend I'm not disappointed. I hear the boss's daughter – '

'The pay's good,' Yorkie interrupted firmly. 'It's cheaper living up there. And plenty of open space.'

'Mm. Own house. Fishing every weekend. Edale on your doorstep. Who can blame you?' The trouble was, he did seem to be blaming Yorkie. 'How long have you been in the Force, Smith? Five years? It takes that long for a copper to become good at the job. Really good. And you're a really good copper. Not the sort of man I like to see turning his back on it.'

Now they tell me, thought Yorkie: now they get round to the compliments instead of the dressings-down and the pushing around. He stood almost to attention, and said: 'Like you say, sir, five years. And what's the point? What have I achieved? What do any of us achieve? No matter how hard we try. We don't change anything, we don't even solve much crime. Seems to me we're only here to clean up the mess. Wipe the blood and the bits away so they don't make the

100

street untidy. Well, I've just had enough of being a social road-sweeper, that's all.'

Conway stood up level with him, his face set. 'Fine. Well, if leaving's right for you then it must be right for us as well, mustn't it?' He held out his hand for a dismissive handshake. 'All the best.'

Yorkie went off to have his breakfast. When he had finished and gone back to front office to see if there were any other forms for him to fill in, or a few odd jobs around to fill in the next few hours, Ted Roach came marching along the corridor waving a plastic bag laden with keys.

'Eighteen sets so far, Yorkie. We're talking a twenty-thousand-pound sting plus ten grand's worth of video tapes. Leave me your address and I'll send you a postcard with the result.'

Peters looked out of the CAD room. 'Yorkie, the very man. Your old flame Mrs Allison's just been on. Granville Street. Reports a prowler on the prowl again. Fancy a last one for luck?'

'What about Reg?'

'On an extended breakfast.' Peters sounded hasty and unconvincing. 'Federation business. Anyway, I do think you ought to pay the old dear a last visit. Give her a chance to weep over you.'

Yorkie stared. The sergeant seemed very anxious to get him off the premises. Maybe they were arranging a surprise for him and wanted him out of the way. Otherwise why was Peters so obviously trying to suppress a grin? It would make better sense for a presentation, if there was going to be one, to take place in the pub. He hoped there wouldn't be.

Probably he was dreaming it all up. And there was something in what Peters said. Old Daisy Allison had been one of his pets: or he had been one of hers. He owed her a visit. At a low ebb over a year ago, facing an AQR interview with Inspector Frazer and with only a few run-of-the-mill collars on his record for a long time, he had needed a breakthrough, and Daisy had provided it. But for Daisy he would never have been put on to the Bright brothers and notched up a winner.

'Right, sarge.'

'Good lad. Take panda two.'

This was something else he would be doing for the last time. He drove along familiar streets, took the short cut down to the end of Granville Street, and slowed to the kerb alongside the familiar terrace of council houses. He knocked at the door of number seventeen.

Mrs Allison opened the door and beamed at him.

Yorkie frowned back. 'Caught you, Daisy! What about the door chain?'

She started fumbling with the chain. 'Oh dear, yes, I forgot to . . . oh, dear.'

'Too late now, love. I'm in, aren't I?'

He walked through, turning automatically into the musty but always tidy parlour. Behind him Daisy Allison fussed with the door chain and then shuffled to the doorway of the parlour.

'Do you know, you're the first person I've spoken to all week.' Her voice was growing thinner and reedier, and her cheeks had become almost transparent. She had always been a cheerful old woman, and the spark was still there; but it was growing dimmer. It was the first time he had heard her sound plaintive, almost peevish. 'You'd like a cup of tea, wouldn't you, dear?'

'Well . . .'

He realised that he was in for a fairly long session. But it was the least he could offer her. And it would be for the last time. When she had brought in the tea tray, shaking alarmingly between her arthritic fingers, Yorkie took out his notebook and made his voice very official and decisive.

'Now, Mrs Allison.'

'You always call me Daisy.'

'Daisy. What's this about a prowler?'

'Been around two or three times lately. Just when it's getting dark, or first thing in the morning. Sometimes he just nips

102

along the other side of the street, having a good look up at these houses. But once I'm sure I heard him out the back, trying the gate into the back yard.'

Yorkie looked around the room at the few ornaments, and the shell souvenir from Margate. There was nothing here worth nicking. But there had been plenty of crazy thefts in the district, and two cases of old women being brutally beaten simply because they didn't have anything worth stealing.

'Can you describe him?'

'Well, he was young. Sort of early twenties, you know. And he was wearing those scruffy blue trousers they all wear nowadays.'

'Jeans?'

'That's it. And a dark blue anorak.'

Scrupulously Yorkie noted down all the details, though none of them added up to anything special. Then, over the second cup of tea, he told Daisy that this would be his last visit. She did not really take it in the first time. Then, as Peters had predicted, tears welled up into her eyes. He patted her hand. Daisy wept even more, then wiped her eyes and began to work up an interest. So little happened to her nowadays: she was eager for the whole story of where he was going, and what he would be doing, and was he going to get married and would he ever bring his wife back here to see her?

When he got up to leave she began to sniff again, but scurried out into the kitchen and returned with a large piece of fruit cake wrapped in a folded paper bag.

'Here you are, dear. It'll be good for you.'

Perhaps she had a vision of him driving away from her door and heading this very minute non-stop for Yorkshire, needing something to eat on the way.

As he unlatched the chain of the front door, she said: 'What's our new man like?'

'Oh, he'll be fine. You'll see.'

'Should I ask for him by name?'

Yorkie gulped. 'Well, yes, you do that, love. Reg Hollis.' He felt that he was betraying her. This final day was not the

103

agreeable wind-down he had been hoping for. Everyone seemed to be doing their best to load him with feelings of guilt. But at least Hollis was always glad of an excuse to grab free tea and cake, and wouldn't mind listening to old Daisy at great length if it kept him away from real work.

As he turned for a final goodbye, she said: 'No car today?'

He stared at the kerb where he had left the panda. The space was bare. There was no police car or, now he looked, any other sort of car in the street. He felt in his pocket. The keys were still there, and he knew he had locked the car before going up to Daisy Allison's door. Yet somebody had managed to drive it away.

Now he had real cause to feel guilty. On his very last day he had managed to lose an official vehicle.

Ten

'Well,' said Sergeant Peters over the R/T, 'that wasn't very clever, was it, Yorkie?' He made it sound a great big joke; which it certainly was not for PC, soon to be ex-PC, Smith. The ex-PC bit was fine. But at the moment he was still on the strength, and still liable.

It made no sense. Despairingly he repeated what he had already told them. 'I know I locked it. I've still got the keys.'

'You can't drive a set of keys, Smith.' Peters was sounding a whole lot tougher. 'You'd better leg it back to the nick and be quick about it. I'll put out an all-units.'

Yorkie set off on the humiliating march back to Sun Hill. It was all very well trying to tell himself that tomorrow he would be free of all this, wouldn't give a damn. Tomorrow would be a great day. Today was turning out to be anything but a great day. As he walked he stared vainly down every side turning and even down alleys too narrow for any vehicle wider than a pushbike. Nobody who nicked a police car could expect to get very far. What chilled his blood was the thought that maybe they had worked it all out and didn't intend to be using it for very long anyway: some brief smash-and-grab, or a gangland hit-and-run, and that would be it. Ditch the car, and be done with it. Courtesy of PC Yorkie Smith, leaving the Force of his own free will just before he earned dismissal under a cloud.

Beside a line of lock-up garages he saw two youths with their heads together, and something was changing hands. It had nothing to do with a panda car, and nothing to do with a policeman on the verge of retirement. But all at once Yorkie

105

was wide awake again. His mind clocked what was going on, and he sprinted down the lane beside the garages.

One of the young men got a warning of his approach, squeaked something, and made a dash for the far end of the lane. He had vanished by the time Yorkie reached the other seedy lout, scrabbling on the ground for a small packet that had been thrown to one side in the flight. He was poised to lob it into a nearby drain when Yorkie caught his arm.

'Give it here. Let's have it.'

'Get yer own.'

Yorkie had secured his arm, and squeezed until the packet dropped into his free hand. Then he recognised this captive.

'Andy Bradwell! You stupid little prat.' He turned the packet over in his palm. 'The hard stuff now, is it?'

'Goin' up in the world, in' I?' Bradwell tried to brazen it out.

'You reckon? You wanna take a good look in the mirror, son.' Yorkie pinned Bradwell against a garage door with one hand while he dipped his head towards his radio. It was not difficult to hold the seedy little runt steady. 'Sierra Oscar from 148. Receiving? Over.'

Sergeant Peters replied. 'Have you found it, Yorkie?'

'No, I haven't found it,' snapped Yorkie. 'But what I have found is Andy Bradwell trading drugs, and I'd like some transport for us, please.'

'Bradwell again? What's he after – a place in the Guinness Book of Records?'

Looking at the pallid face and its uncontrollable tic, Yorkie doubted if the kid was likely to live long enough for that. He wondered how long it was since Bradwell, busy passing the stuff to others, had had his own last fix. A London riddled with plague carriers like Andy Bradwell was a place he'd be glad to be out of.

The car came quickly enough. Melvin, driving it, was polite enough not to comment on another car that had mysteriously gone missing. It was the first time Yorkie had appreciated the value of Melvin's religiously charitable convictions.

As he led Andy Bradwell into the custody area, PC Tony Stamp was perched on a corner of Sergeant Penny's desk, holding forth. 'It's still a cop-out, isn't it? A cushy little number with your ex-bird's father, instead of taking the flak where it really hurts.'

'Yorkie's an idealist.' Penny shrugged in his easygoing way. 'They really believe what they read in the recruitment bumf. So they're always the first to get worn down.'

'A frigging good job we're not all idealists then.'

Yorkie waited for Sergeant Penny to notice him, but it was Stamp who reacted first.

'Oh, hello there, Yorkie. I hear you lost your motor.'

'Yeah, but not me bottle, right?' He shoved Bradwell towards the charge room, with Penny in leisurely pursuit. 'Possession and possible dealing, Sarge.'

'Surprise, surprise.' Penny handed over a bunch of keys, arousing a faint shudder in Yorkie as he remembered an earlier collection of keys that very day. 'Stick him in the detention cell and let CID know. And make sure you give me chapter and verse before you throw away your pocket-book.'

Yorkie grimly escorted the prisoner to cell three, and jerked a thumb to indicate that he should go in.

'Enjoy yourself,' said Bradwell, the spitefulness eating outwards through the twitch of his withdrawal symptoms. As the cell door clanged shut, he screeched out: 'Mr Pig.'

Sergeant Cryer nodded at Smith as he passed. 'The lasting memory, eh, Yorkie?'

Beyond Cryer was the substantial figure of Chief Superintendent Brownlow. 'My office in half an hour, Smith.'

Yorkie's heart sank. He had known there would be trouble about the missing vehicle, but had not anticipated that the trouble would come down in a great thunder from the very top.

Brownlow added: 'Our farewell chat, right?'

'Oh . . . yes, right, sir.'

At a loose end, Yorkie drifted into the CAD room. Peters was at his desk, and Cryer was sorting out papers on one corner of it. Whatever they had been saying, they stopped abruptly as Yorkie arrived.

'Any joy, sarge?' he asked.

Peters shook his head gravely. 'Not so much as a skid mark, son.'

It was too much. Did the whole lot of them, on an all-units alert, drive about with their eyes shut, or what?

Peters was chatting to Bob Cryer. 'We haven't lost a motor since Charlie Kerr. Remember old Charlie? Mind you, he used to park that Morris Minor of his outside the pub. Not surprising it went walkabout. Lost his pension over it. Still' – Peters beamed over Cryer's shoulder – 'that won't worry you, will it, Yorkie?'

Sergeant Cryer was shaking his head now. It was becoming a habit in here. 'Gonna look a bit sick on his inventory this afternoon, though.'

Yorkie was at the end of his tether. 'Oh, come off it, sarge.'

'Too true,' Peters contributed. 'Dead right. I mean, when you hand in your gear . . . I mean, Stores can swallow the odd missing pair of trousers. But a patrol car . . .'

It was no good. He was grinning too broadly. And Sergeant Cryer was not daring to look straight at Yorkie.

There was a sniggering from the corridor. Suspicions of a wind-up began at last to dawn on Yorkie before he had turned to see Tony Stamp and Taffy Edwards lounging in the doorway. Stamp pulled a set of car keys out of his pocket and dangled them on his little finger, raised in Yorkie's direction.

Yorkie flung himself at the pair of them. They disappeared into the nearest room, Cathy Marshall's ILO territory, with Yorkie Smith crashing after them and yelling at the top of his voice. 'You poxy pair of toe-rags – where is it?' He came face to face not with his tormentors but with Chief Superintendent Brownlow, moving away from one of the filing cabinets, and skidded to a breathless halt.

Brownlow said mildly: 'Winding down, Smith? Perhaps we ought to have our little chat now, if you've nothing better to do.'

'Yes, sir.'

Stamp and Edwards stood solemnly to one side as Yorkie followed the Chief Superintendent out of the room and up the stairs to the first-floor corridor. As they reached his office, his secretary came out.

'Excuse me, sir. Councillor Wainwright's arrived for his pre-lunch meeting.'

'Already?' Brownlow looked slightly thrown, but immediately recovered himself. His limp smile at Yorkie showed at once that between the influential local councillor and the departing constable, there was really no contest. 'Sorry, Smith. Perhaps later.' He hastily shook hands. 'If not, let me say how sorry I am you're leaving. You will of course be given a satisfactory reference.'

'Thank you, sir.'

Thanks a bunch, Yorkie added to himself as he headed back towards the stairs he had so recently climbed.

Bob Cryer, emerging from the CID office, looked surprised. 'That was quick.'

'I think it said everything, sarge.'

They descended together in silence. In the front office Cryer began to look more cheerful. 'By the way, your panda's in the yard behind the transit.'

'Never had you down as a wind-up, sarge.'

'Getting reckless in my old age. Besides, not every day we lose a Yorkie Smith. I could name a few I'd like to lose,' Cryer grunted, 'but they're the ones who hang on forever. Anyway, while you're here . . .' He took a property book from the shelf, checked an entry, and went on: 'Don't forget to clear your corres tray. And don't walk off with your warrant card. Tell Peak Security to issue their own. Oh, and you've sent your Reason for Leaving questionnaire up the road, have you?'

'Yes.'

'Put in the bit about the social road-sweeper, did you?'

Startled by this bit of inside knowledge, Yorkie forced an awkward smile. 'Yes I did, actually.'

'Good.' Cryer said it fervently and obviously meant it. 'Don't suppose the prats up there will have a clue what you're talking about, but good.'

Ted Roach looked for the twentieth time at the dashboard clock, and swore. He wanted to have this thing wrapped up and be on his way to the *Grapes* to make sure of Yorkie Smith getting a worthy send-off. But the Coopers were obstinately refusing to show up and put him out of his misery. He might as well have assigned Dashwood or Jimmy Carver to this boring watch. But he had somehow made a bet with himself that he could dig out the truth of this one within ten minutes of meeting the Coopers.

Earlier this morning the woman in the neighbouring flat had said they were due back from Spain any minute. 'But you know what those flights are like, and the way you're always kept waiting at Heathrow.' He knew; but he still calculated that they ought to be able to make it around lunchtime. Then he would have some questions to ask about the money that had paid for their nice jaunt to Spain.

Certainly they were not short of a bob or two. This block of flats with its entry phone and the flower-boxes along its front balconies was no great distance from certain other high-rise blocks he could mention, but in a lot of ways it was in another world.

If they didn't show up within the next half-hour, he was going to call it a day. Yorkie's booze-up was a lot more important than the shifty dealings of a couple of con-artists.

Just as Roach was about to pull away under the trim line of trees along the boulevard, a black taxi closed in ahead of him. A middle-aged couple got out. Their suntan suggested Spain as a distinct possibility. He waited until they had removed their holiday luggage and the man was paying off the cabbie, and then got out and sauntered towards them.

'Mr and Mrs Cooper?'

'Yes.'

'Owners of the video shop in Kilby Street?'

Mrs Cooper did not look the least bit apprehensive. On the contrary: she exchanged a quick, hopeful smile with her husband. 'Why, do you want to buy it?'

'Don't you think you've sold it to enough people already, madam?'

Within less than a minute he realised that the remark had been well and truly out of order. Fortunately Cooper did not seem to get the meaning, and was genuinely too concerned with the facts to take offence. After Roach had communicated the news that the shop was utterly empty and that their business neighbour, Mr Shah, had reported possible burglars, Cooper picked up two of the bags and led the way towards the main entrance to the flats. Co-opted into carrying a third bag, Roach panted out a few basic details as they crossed the narrow hall, and a few more as they went up in the lift.

Mrs Cooper let out a sigh at their front door. 'So all the stock's gone?'

'Every last little Rambo reel.'

Inside the flat, Roach was offered a large, plushy armchair while Cooper dug into an airport bag and began extracting various bottles of duty-free.

'Well, thank God it's only the shop.' Mrs Cooper, perhaps suffering after-holiday lag, was remarkably philosophical. 'I thought you were going to tell us the flat had been burgled, or the water bed slashed. That's my one worry with it, you know: a puncture . . . all those tons of water. Still, they're very strongly constructed.'

She looked round the room with proprietorial pride. If you had to come home from foreign delights, this was the place to come to. Everything was expensive. Even to Roach's uncritical eye a lot of it was in pretty poor, gaudy taste; but there was no denying that a lot of money had been spent on it, just to make it clear that money was not in short supply.

He said: 'Mrs Cooper, it's the shop all right, but we're not just talking about a straightforward burglary.'

'What else could it be?'

'D'you know a Mr and Mrs Durban?'

'Durban?' She shook her head. 'Eric, do we know anyone called Durban?'

Cooper was lovingly shifting a litre bottle of Spanish brandy in the direction of a brass-studded drinks cabinet. 'Nope.'

'We know some Dunbars,' Mrs Cooper mused. 'Jane and Roy.'

'Old friends? Business partners?' said Roach hopefully.

'Oh, *them*.' Cooper closed the door of the cabinet. 'No, we thought we'd be doing business, got very matey for a while, you know how it is. Jane and Roy, Millie and Sam, the lot. They wanted to take over the shop earlier this year. Then they pulled out.'

Roach wriggled in the armchair, finding it difficult to sit up and free himself from its plump embrace. He was pretty sure he knew the answer to his next question before he asked it. 'When you say they pulled out, did they ever have keys to the shop?'

'They must have done. Yes, of course they did.'

'They ran it a week or two to get the hang of it,' his wife chimed in, 'while the new lease was being drawn up for them. Then about a month ago they suddenly said they'd changed their minds, gave us back the keys, and that was it.' She thought for a moment. 'Just before we went on holiday. Said something about moving to Scotland, didn't they, Eric?'

'That's right. Scotland.'

Roach gave a rueful little sigh, and made a great effort to lever himself up from the chair. There was nothing else to be done here. He was not sure there was much to be done anywhere else: nothing of any real use.

As he went back into Sun Hill, Stamp and Melvin were on their way out. Their destination was obvious. So was their haste to get there. Roach tapped Stamp on the shoulder. 'Get me one in.' He hurried past the public waiting area, only to be stopped in his tracks by a glum-looking couple on one of the benches. He recognised them as Sherry and Mick Broome. There was no telling how long they had been sitting here waiting for news. Their hopeful expressions as they saw

Roach faded when he told them the truth, making it short and brutal because there was no other way. They had been conned. It was a very clever little con, and they and all the others had been done up like kippers. Of course the police would pursue their enquiries, and would keep them informed. But Roach's expression told them how little chance they had of ever getting their money back. He shrugged his apologies, and went along the corridor for a quick spruce-up session in the washroom.

Behind him he caught the wail of Sherry Broome's bitter lament: 'They're all the same. None of 'em gives a toss.'

All you could do with a remark like that was let it drift away over your head. If Sun Hill had ever set about making an official collection of such summings-up by the general public, Cathy Marshall's office would have had to be trebled in size.

'Us caring coppers,' said Reg Hollis, 'we're on a hiding to nothing.'

The locker room was seething with PCs changing from uniform into civvies, most of them changing more quickly than usual so that they could dash across the road and get stuck in. But Hollis's remark caused a moment of incredulous stillness.

'You?' said Yorkie Smith. 'A caring copper?'

'Us caring coppers,' Hollis went on, oblivious, 'are the salt of the earth, but like I said, we're on a hiding to nothing.'

'Put him in your suitcase, Yorkie, for God's sake.'

'So don't get me wrong, Yorkie.' There was no stopping Hollis. 'As Federation rep I fully appreciate your reasons for leaving. But also as Federation rep there's no way I can approve of you moving into the private sector.'

'I'm not asking you to approve, mate.'

'I mean, these security firms ain't just patrolling building sites and factories now, are they? Or just swanning around in a van with a load of Christmas parcels. It's shopping centres, even housing estates. Specially up north. It's the thin end of the privatisation wedge.'

113

Taffy Edwards shrugged into a bright check shirt. 'You can hardly blame folk for employing a firm to protect their property if the police can't manage it, can you?'

'But they're paying twice for the same service, ain't they?'

'What service? If I lived in a street that had twelve break-ins a week, I know what I'd feel about the police.'

'That's not our fault, is it?' Haynes objected.

'I never said it was.'

'What d'you expect with plonkers at the top and a government that wants the job run like ICI?'

'The Guardian Angels?' said Haynes slyly.

That started Hollis off on another tack. 'Yeh, well, that's another thing, isn't it? Vigilantes – '

'I bet that's really why Yorkie's off to Sheffield or wherever,' grinned Haynes. 'He's going to start his own chapter – patrolling empty pubs.'

'You'll ponce a drink off me before I go, though, won't you?' said Yorkie.

'Course I'll ponce a drink off you. What do you think I am, an idealist?'

'And why are we nattering in here, when there's much nicer lecture rooms not three hundred yards away? Come on, let's get moving.'

They got moving, all except for Yorkie himself, who was tidying up the last visible remnants of his police career. Along the corridor and out into the street, Edwards took up the theme with an intensity that might have had something to do with envy over Yorkie's departure, or simply a leftover from disciplinary criticism levelled at him regularly by Sergeant Cryer. 'It's not just the government though, is it now? The local council clobbers you every time you try to do the job, and then there's all the top brass in the nick on to you, and Joe Public thinks it's all our fault anyway.'

'You leaving too then, Taff? Back to them green Welsh hills?'

'And the grey Welsh dole queues? No thanks.' But there

had been the suspicion of a pause before he tossed the question over his shoulder out of sight.

'How about a transfer, then?' Haynes persisted. 'You could buy a five-bedroom house in Wales on a copper's salary.'

'What would I want with a five-bedroom house?'

Left behind in the locker room, Yorkie Smith patted the pockets of his sports jacket and fastened the middle button. Methodically he folded his uniform trousers and added them to the neat pile of uniform he had stacked on a chair. For a moment he was at a loss. Then he reached for his helmet and cap, balanced them on top, and walked slowly past the rows of lockers towards the door. It took only a few minutes to hand them over to the girl in Stores, who ticked them off on a list, gave him a receipt, and smiled.

And that was that. Except for the farewell party across the road. He had been looking forward to it. Now he was not so sure.

They seemed to have been doing very nicely without him. As he pushed the door of the saloon bar open there was such a racket that nobody noticed him right away. A group around Taffy Edwards were already halfway through their first clutch of pints. Sergeant Cryer was crouched over the counter at the far end, holding forth to someone unseen. Tony Stamp was pushing an empty tankard towards the barmaid with a cursory 'On Yorkie Smith's slate, love' before continuing his own bit of holding forth.

'I love the job as well, you know. You don't have to be one of the caring coppers, whatever that might mean. You've just got to like nicking people, because at the end of the day it's very simple. Five per cent of the population is slag, and it's our job to keep that five per cent under the thumb.'

Sergeant Cryer raised his head, either to put in a word of agreement or to slap the whole idea down, and saw Smith in the doorway. He moved across with his hand out, put his arm round Yorkie like a loving uncle, and drew him into the middle of the uproar.

'About time, too. There's somebody here looking for you.'

'Y'what?'

'That way. There's one or two blokes not here yet, but she says she can't wait.'

'Now just a minute, sarge . . .' Yorkie was suspicious about any further wind-ups after what had happened earlier in the day. This could be a kissagram, or anything. With this lot, you could always fear the worst.

A space was being cleared in the middle of the saloon bar. Into the centre of it hobbled an elderly lady with wisps of grey hair straggling from under her bonnet. She was leaning on a walking stick, and glanced from one side to the other as if for reassurance. Sergeant Cryer, with a gallantry nobody had ever observed before, patted her affectionately on the shoulder.

She drew herself up within the folds of her long, voluminous brown coat.

'PC Smith.' Her voice was as thin and quavery as Daisy Allison's had been. 'On behalf of all the old ladies on the manor that you've been so kind to . . . and fitted us all with such lovely door chains, Mrs Allison and Mrs Singleton and all the rest of us, I'd just like to say . . .' Her voice cracked with emotion, and there was a murmur of sympathy around the bar. 'Just like to say . . .' She moved with painful slowness closer to Yorkie, and dropped her stick. Just as he was about to stoop and pick it up, she flung open her coat and slid it from her shoulders. They were very smooth, glowing shoulders. The rest of her, emerging from a skimpy covering of pink satin underwear, was just as smooth and, as Yorkie discovered when she clasped him to her, very warm and sweet-smelling.

There was a roar of applause. As the girl pulled away from him, Yorkie saw that she had a dazzling smile to garnish all the rest – and it was the smile of WPC Claire Brind. They were all slapping him on the back, and Claire darted forward again and gave him a kiss, and somebody was shoving a pint glass at him, and looking at Claire Brind's shape he wondered

116

if . . . whether . . . if maybe he had decided not to go, then maybe . . .

'Come on, Yorkie. You've got some serious drinking ahead. Don't just stand there.'

It was genuine friendship, and he would miss it. But the decision had been made, and it was the right one, and there was no going back now. He took a last quick glance at Claire and then tried to thrust unworthy, treacherous thoughts from his mind.

All the same, he was sorry when she wrapped the coat round herself again.

Eleven

She was cutting things a bit fine. Half an hour ago there had seemed to be plenty of time to park the car, nip into the supermarket, and do some brisk shopping before reporting for afternoon parade at Sun Hill. But WPC Norika Datta had not counted on an ageing woman in the checkout queue ahead of her, waiting until all the items in a whole trolley-load of groceries had been rung up at the till before even beginning to fumble with her bag, groping for a purse right at the bottom, and then finding that she couldn't get the last little bits of change out from its corners. When Norika could not repress a worried little gasp of impatience, the woman turned, looked her up and down, and then stared meaningly into her golden Asian face and nodded knowingly. If Norika had been in uniform, the sneer would probably have been even more marked.

Getting into uniform before parade was going to be one mad scramble. As she reached the car park and sprinted towards the Fiesta, there were only ten minutes to go before she was due on parade.

Then the car refused to start.

It was sickening. Quite apart from the sort of reception she could expect from the duty sergeant, she hated being late. Too many people expected a girl like her to be just that bit lazier than most, just that bit likelier to yawn and slow down and not bother; which was why she made a point of getting everything done strictly according to the book, on time, and all tidy and correct.

She flipped the release catch and scrambled out to hoist the bonnet. Not that there was much point in inspecting the engine, really: she had no idea how it worked or what could have made it go wrong.

'Problems, love?'

She jerked upright, almost catching her head on the rim of the bonnet. A mild man in his late forties, with an unbuttoned light brown raincoat and a shabby cardigan, was standing a few feet away. Under his tweed cap the expression behind his glasses was neither pushy nor mildly condescending at the state she was in. His smile was awkward and deferential, as if accosting young women in public places was something he was not used to.

'I'm late,' she said dismally, 'and it's completely dead.'

'Not even turning over?'

'Nothing.'

He peered under the bonnet. 'Get in and try again. Let's have a listen.'

Norika got back in and turned the key again. Still there was nothing. The dashboard clock was still remorselessly working, though: the minute hand was creeping towards 2.00 pm.

The man said: 'It's your start relay switch.' He came to stand by the driver's door. 'You won't move without a new one.'

'Oh, great.'

'You with the RAC or anyone?'

'No.'

'Not to worry.' He smiled feeble condolences. 'If you've got twenty pounds, that's all a switch costs. They do them in the auto shop round the corner.'

'Yes, but I wouldn't know how . . .'

'Look, miss, I'll do it if you like. Only a three-minute job.' Before she could protest he raised his hand. 'Stay with your car.'

There was not much else she could do. After he had gone she looked wretchedly at the clock and then at her watch, trying to make one of them contradict the other in her favour. At the same time she tried to calculate how long it would take to walk to Sun Hill, knowing just how little chance she had of

119

splashing out money on a taxi in this part of the world. After a minute and a half she was already convinced the man, who had looked pretty absent-minded anyway, had forgotten her and simply wandered off. Probably another one of them: one of those who thought girls with her background and appearance could only be a bad joke, a blot on the English landscape, to be treated at best as kids and then ignored. Kept her waiting just for the fun of it, even if it was difficult for anyone else to see what was funny about it.

This little episode was going to lead to some snide remarks when she did at last get to the station.

Nobody had ever put it to her in so many words, but Norika had suspected from the start that she had been taken on as a 'token ethnic'. She had not even sought the job. Her father, a doctor with a practice on the other side of the river, had had a patient who knew a social worker who knew an inspector in charge of a recruiting drive, and somehow it had all come to pass. She had few complaints, basically: or would have had none if the Sun Hill lot had not been so well schooled in giving her nothing to complain about. Sergeant Cryer had gone out of his way to treat her with a courtesy which was sometimes almost too obvious. With him, though, it was genuine. She was not so sure about some of the others. When she had brought in one of the brawniest troublemakers on the manor, doubled up in agony, without even needing to call radio for assistance, Claire Brind had wonderingly asked about her knowledge of mysterious eastern tortures. Actually her technique had derived simply from her knowledge of her father's essays in the BMJ on pressure points, when she had helped him with the paperwork.

Still there was always that uncertainty. She was tempted every now and then to assure the rest of them that there was uncertainty on both sides: whatever doubts they had about her, she had just about as many doubts about them, too.

Relief surged up within her as her Good Samaritan plodded back across the car park floor, waving a cellophane packet whose contents meant nothing to her. He looked brighter and

120

more energetic now, perhaps relishing the thought of doing his good deed for the day.

'Make sure you're switched off.' He ducked under the bonnet again. From where she sat it was impossible to make out what he was doing, but it did not take long. 'Okay, try her now.'

She turned the key. The engine sprang into life at once. After the engine had ticked over for a few seconds, the man slammed down the bonnet and came back to her.

'That's great,' she gasped. Now it was her turn to fumble for her bag. 'How much was it?'

'Twenty-one fifty including VAT.' He waved a crumpled slip of paper.

She thrust five fivers at him. 'Please get yourself a drink as well.'

'No, no, that's far too much.'

'Please. I'd have been stranded otherwise. I'm really so grateful. Goodbye.'

He stepped back, smiling and clutching the notes, as she drove off in a wild arc towards the exit slope.

At the station she hesitated between trying to scramble into uniform or getting to parade to miss as little as possible; and opted for the parade. Hurrying along the corridor, she heard the buzz of voices from within the LIO room, and apprehensively opened the door.

Sergeant Penny, clipboard in hand, was taking parade. As she slid in he was saying: 'Main thing this afternoon, will you welcome, please, PC Dave Quinnan, who after two years at Bow Street has transferred here to learn how the job should be done.'

The new arrival had dark wavy hair, thrusting shoulders, and a brash, thick-lipped smile. He was good-looking in an aggressive, macho way, and from the angle at which Norika Datta caught him he appeared well satisfied with himself.

'I'm tailing Rich, actually.' He was very loud and boisterous as he nodded towards PC Richard Turnham. 'Commissioner's orders.'

'Both at Bow Street together, I hear?' Sergeant Penny looked briefly benevolent. 'A friendly face among strangers, then.'

Richard Turnham's smile was one of wary acknowledgement; not what most people would have called friendly.

'Right, then.' Penny turned his attention back to the clipboard. '572 Garfield on panda three. 226 Martella, front desk.'

'Er, Sarge.' It was Reg Hollis. Penny, who hated to be interrupted, glared at him; but Hollis was impervious to that sort of thing. 'Sarge, who was the bloke nosing around the nick this morning?'

'Bloke?' Penny was mystified. 'Nosing around the nick?'

'Yeh.' Hollis was delighted that he knew something the sergeant did not. 'Terry Beavis in Traffic tells me there was a bloke looking in rooms. Only if he was from the Inspectorate I'd like to point out, as Federation rep . . .'

'He wasn't from the Inspectorate, Hollis.' It was Inspector Frazer, in the far corner of the room. 'He was from Estate Management.'

'Oh. Thank you, ma'am.' Hollis made a last attempt. 'Would you happen to know what he was doing?'

'Managing the estate, I expect.'

Penny continued. 'Dave' – he raised an eyebrow in the newcomer's direction – 'I was sending you out with WPC Datta on five beat, but as she seems not to be gracing us with her presence, we'll hold fire on that.'

'Er, sarge . . .' Norika Datta's voice was croaky and indistinct.

Inspector Frazer frowned across the room, and Penny produced a scowl over the top of the clipboard. 'I haven't got you down for plain clothes duty.'

'No, I'm sorry, sergeant. I was late so I thought I'd better just – '

'Hardly a good example to set to a new colleague.' Before she could blunder on with her apologies, he waved his hand to block any further discussion, and finished off the allocation of duties. 'Oh, and one more thing. Information from Barton Street. Apparently our old chum the bogus repair man has

122

been working local patches again. Varying descriptions, but basically white, middle-aged, medium height, and looks respectable. For those of you who are not familiar, this is a very plausible gentleman who haunts car parks and disables motors when their owners aren't around, usually by springing the bonnet and disconnecting a wire or two.' Shrinking back against the wall, WPC Datta had an awful feeling inside that she could tell exactly how Penny's account would shape up. 'He then nobly comes to the aid of his unsuspecting victim, reconnects the wires, pockets twenty quid or so for buying the vital new part – which he's had in his pocket all the time in case anyone asks – and walks off with the driver's eternal thanks ringing in his ears.'

'Leave it out, sarge,' groaned Garfield. 'Who'd fall for that?'

'There's one born every minute, Garfield, so you'd better get out on the streets and protect them. And that goes for the rest of you. Off you go.'

Stunned, Norika let them brush past into the corridor, until there were only the new arrival and Sergeant Penny left in the room with her.

Tom Penny said: 'You as well, please. I'm sure PC Quinnan will wait while you get changed. You're showing him five beat.'

She tried to pull herself together. 'Oh, right.' Her smile was on the abstract side. 'Sorry.'

As she turned towards the door she heard Penny say: 'I *was* going to tell you she's shaping up as one of our most reliable officers.'

'That's all right, sarge. Most women go peculiar when they meet me.'

That was enough to shake WPC Datta out of her daze and restore her to full possession of her faculties. Dave Quinnan was not, she felt, going to prove an asset to the Sun Hill team: certainly not much of a substitute for Yorkie Smith.

While Quinnan was waiting in the LIO room for his escort to reappear, Cathy Marshall came in to reclaim her territory. She nodded pleasantly to Quinnan before settling down at her desk and beginning to sort through the crime sheets. Without waiting for an invitation he perched himself on the corner of the desk.

'So you're the collator? Cath is the name, I'm told.'

'That's right.' She did not bother to look up. 'I know everything about everyone, so watch out.'

'Nothing to know in my case. Except I go a bundle on mature women.'

This time she did look up. 'That's a pity,' she said sweetly, 'because I hate cheeky kids.'

She waved him off her desk. He positioned himself in the door for a moment, then took a few paces towards the front office, curious about every last little detail of his new base.

WPC Martella had left the front desk to sit down behind the screen and chat to PC Stamp. Hollis's question about the wandering surveyor, although put in Hollis's usual unlovable and resentful way, had already stirred a few doubts in other folks' minds. Occasionally there had been official statements about modernisation, and once or twice that dread word 'rationalisation' had surfaced, with the possible implication of Sun Hill and Barton Street being combined, or relocated, or absorbed, or whatever choice name the planners cared to put on it.

'Can't help there being a lot of rumour and speculation,' Martella commented.

'Isn't that what police stations are for?'

Martella leaned closer to Stamp. 'One or two people might shift, of course. Got any sense, they'll be out before the blow falls.'

'Such as?'

'Well . . . Frazer, for one. There's been a lot of phone calls, and applications for this, that and the other. Or so I've heard. I mean, it makes sense. You always lose staff in that sort of situation, so it would be the obvious moment for her to be . . .'

Belatedly Martella became aware that Stamp's odd little

124

grimaces at her were not the after-effects of canteen hamburgers. She turned, to find Inspector Frazer crossing front office towards the duty inspector's office.

'Martella.'

'Yes, ma'am.'

'I couldn't help overhearing.' Frazer was quiet and crisp. 'Let's get our rumours right, shall we? I have applied for a course at Bramshill. That has nothing whatsoever to do with a fleeting visit to Sun Hill by an estate surveyor. Understood?'

'Yes, of course, ma'am.'

'You're on the front desk, I believe.'

There was no need for any more to be said. Martella headed back to the front desk. Making sure Frazer was out of the way, Dave Quinnan moved in to intercept her.

'Martella, that's a romantic name. What goes with it: Maria . . . Rosita?'

'Viv.'

'Oh, very nice.' He reached for her left hand and gave a little nod. 'Just checking marital status. I like to know where I am before I start.'

'You're at the back of a very long queue.' Viv leaned over the desk to await an elderly man who had just puffed in through the main door.

Stamp, enjoying the spectacle, said: 'The crumpet here set very high standards, Dave. They're used to quality.'

'Huh!' It was June Ackland, walking purposefully through on her way to the custody area.

'Now crack that one,' Stamp confided, 'and you'd get a cup in the station trophy case.'

WPC Datta appeared, a little breathless, but impeccable in her uniform.

'And her?' Quinnan spoke in an undertone. 'Uh?'

Stamp shook his head dismissively. 'No chance.'

The two of them headed for the corridor towards the rear entrance. June Ackland, hurrying back, stood aside to let them pass.

Quinnan waved back at her. 'See you later – June, isn't it? Buy you tea.'

'Steady on. I take milk and sugar, you know. Cost you a fortune.'

It was a bright day, but with a long streak of grey edging closer from the horizon. Not that you saw much horizon in the neighbourhood of Sun Hill except through gaps between demolished buildings or through the twisted patterns of the traffic flyover. WPC Datta tried to put the disagreeable memory of the early afternoon out of her mind and concentrate on explaining the features of the beat to her companion. He did not look too impressed. Clearly things here struck him as being a lot tamer than they had been at Bow Street. The trouble was, in spite of all her effects she could not drag her mind away from the picture of that car park and that diffident, plausible man who had taken her for a ride – if that was the way to put it. She cut a few corners on the regular beat in order to cross the large car park behind the shopping precinct, and the one on rough ground below the railway embankment.

At last Quinnan protested. They had climbed to the top of the multi-storey block overlooking a tangle of terraces due to come down within the next twelve months, and Quinnan was leaning on the wall staring out. 'No disrespect, Norika, but isn't there anything else to five beat except car parks? I mean, I applaud your hundred-per-cent attitude, but this con guy's a nondescript. Unless we catch him in the act we've got no chance.'

'I just feel we'll know him if we see him.'

He glanced at her speculatively. 'What's he gonna have, then: a big label on his forehead?'

She did not dare to give too much away, but it was going to be difficult to force herself to steer them back on to other features of the patrol when they descended.

'Oh, all right.' It was a shrug of defeat, though deep down inside she felt too vengeful to admit defeat.

Quinnan leaned on the parapet and looked down. 'It's only a job after all, love. Does you no good to get too personally involved in it.' Unexpectedly he took out a tube of wine gums and offered it. She took one, and he resumed his contemplation of the sprawl below. 'Doesn't look a bad sort of ground from up here. Even the natives seem friendly.' He was waving to somebody. 'Easily amused, but friendly.'

She moved to the parapet beside him. In the street below a boy and girl were waving vigorously. Dave Quinnan flapped his right hand again. Faintly a voice drifted up to them.

Norika Datta stiffened. The cry was decidedly one of 'Help!'

They glanced at each other, then headed fast for the stairs down to the ground floor.

It would not have surprised either of them to find that the kids, sniggering, had cleared off. But the two were still there, a boy and a girl, ready to call at them as they crossed the road.

'There's a man.'

'Down here, look.'

The girl was urging them towards the opening of a narrow alley. Norika headed after her, only to have her arm caught by Dave Quinnan.

'Easy, now. Could be trouble.'

He edged past her and led the way.

'On the ground,' said the girl. 'Over there, see?'

A man was sprawled on the damp flags of the alley, face down. Quinnan approached cautiously, waving the children to stand back. He stooped and turned the prone figure over on to one side. The man's face was badly cut and swollen, with a red gash ripped across the cheek from his mouth. As Quinnan moved him he groaned and tried to clutch his side, as if his ribs had been badly mauled.

'What happened to you, mate?'

'Who's speaking?' It was no more than a thin, fearful whisper.

'Police.'

'I can't see you.'

A hand crept quaveringly up Quinnan's arm to touch the number on his shoulder. At the same time the little girl darted forward, eagerly showing the policeman something. In her hands were the broken pieces of a white stick.

Twelve

It was not the way Taffy Edwards would have chosen to spend a day off. Even at the last moment he had his doubts and was tempted to turn round and drive away. Instead, he parked his car a discreet distance from the little cluster of maisonettes, where no obvious connection would be noticed in the unlikely event of one of the Sun Hill patrols ranging this far from their regular patch, and walked back to ring the doorbell in the middle of the block. Waiting for an answer, he tugged at the jacket of his lightweight brown suit and made sure the pocket flaps were straight, as if he were still wearing uniform. Furtively he glanced along the street, not wanting to be kept waiting too long on the step.

The man who opened the door was thickset, in his forties, with a crushing handshake but a straightforward hospitable smile. In shirtsleeves and with a loosely knotted tie, he was a lot less formal than his visitor.

'Hello. Er . . . Francis Edwards. PC Edwards.' Taffy had not known what to expect, but somehow had not envisaged quite such a bluff, obvious, ex-CID type: Burnside with an unmalicious smile.

'Ian Mills, Welfare Officer. Come on in.'

It was too late to turn back now. He was ushered through a small hallway into a room equipped with magazines and two of this morning's papers, rather like a dentist's waiting-room.

'You're early,' said Mills cheerfully. 'Must be keen.'

Edwards managed a smile. 'Not really. I wasn't sure how long it would take to get here.'

'Just make yourself comfortable. It'll only be a couple of minutes while I finish off my previous appointment.'

Even more like a dental surgery, thought Edwards glumly. You were given time to reflect on past sins and omissions before you went in and opened your mouth wide, to be told about the shocking neglect of your teeth for which you were shamefully responsible, and then suffer the well-deserved wrenching and drilling which you had brought on yourself.

He felt too fidgety to stay seated. Standing in front of a fireplace with an unlit gas fire, he looked into a painting of what he supposed to be a Scottish glen. Or maybe it was a Welsh lake, or even a Yorkshire one – the kind Yorkie Smith could now stroll round on his days off. It had never been one of Taffy Edwards' ambitions to spend the rest of his life in surroundings like that.

Now he knew there was going to have to be a choice, though half of him rebelled against any such notion. He was not ready for it. The question was whether Sun Hill would soon make the decision for him. There was still a bad aftertaste of that warehouse robbery where he had overlooked so many things and dismissed the owner's worries as 'just another false alarm'. Sergeant Cryer had taken the opportunity to berate him for a host of other misdemeanours, and he had been hauled up in front of Conway for a further battering. Late for duty, refusal to adapt, skiving off to ring the missus (if only they knew the trouble there would be if he didn't!), and inability to stand up to everyday stress. Everyday stress: they could use terms like that without ever considering that there were other stresses, quite outside the job, which did the job no good at all.

Then he had made the mistake of blowing his top when Conway suggested seeing a counsellor. 'I'm happy where I am, and I don't want to discuss anything with anybody.'

Yet here he was; only he was not going to let any of them know that he had come here.

Within five minutes Mills came to collect him and take him through to the counselling room, which was at least furnished with easy chairs rather than a dentist's chair. Against one wall

129

was a table with a coffee percolator and cups. It was all meant to put the patient at ease.

Taffy Edwards perched ill-at-ease on the edge of one of the armchairs.

'Well, now.' Having poured two cups of coffee, Mills settled himself and beamed a practised smile. 'Have you ever been counselled before, Francis?'

'No, never.'

'Well, it's totally confidential, if you've got any lingering worries about that. Nobody's going to know about it unless you tell them. Nobody at Sun Hill, governors or mates. And nobody up the road.'

Edwards would not have ventured to come here if he had thought otherwise. He was not that desperate. Or was he? He sipped at his coffee. His hands began to shake and he had to use both of them for a moment to hold the cup steady.

Mills picked up a notebook. 'I'd like to make a few notes as we go along, if you don't mind. Just so I can refresh my memory before our next session.'

'Next?'

'Oh, yes. Today's the ice-breaker. Usually we like to set up a series of meetings at regular intervals. Sometimes half a dozen – it depends.'

'That won't be necessary,' said Edwards hastily. 'As far as I'm concerned this is a one-off.'

Mills stared knowingly at his notebook as if he had heard this one before and had jotted it down more than once. 'Sorry, no magic wands. Our experience is that the counselling process takes time.'

'I'm not looking for a shoulder to cry on, you know.'

'Of course not.' At least there was not the trace of a patronising note in Mills voice. 'And I'm not intending to spout advice. I'm here to listen, and hopefully help a bit.'

Edwards was beginning to feel prickly about the whole thing. 'So, what's *your* background? I mean, who am I talking to?'

'I'm an ex-detective sergeant, twenty years in the job. So I know it couldn't have been easy for you to phone. Asking for counselling? Wrong image. We're all such tough guys in the Met, aren't we? But that attitude's changing.'

'Look,' said Edwards belligerently, 'I've got no hang-up about being a macho man, all right?'

'Glad to hear it.'

'I just don't . . . well, I don't like talking about myself.'

'But you're here.'

'Yes.'

'So let's talk.'

It came slowly at first, and came out very confused. On the way here Taffy Edwards had rehearsed the things he wanted to confide and the questions he wanted to ask. Now he seemed to have lost the thread of it all, and grabbed at one thing after another at random, just as it surfaced in his mind.

For a while he dodged the issue of slackness, or being accused of it. Then a sour comment of Bob Cryer's slipped out, and he could see that Mills had picked it up and was storing it away for later reference if necessary. Veering away, Edwards went on to describe some of the problems of his marriage: no accusations, no miseries, just an account of how he had got married two years ago to a girl from Wales, and how it had been great at the start, but now there were practical difficulties. The job and Mary didn't go together. Marriage and being a copper didn't mix. Especially when you had a wife who was beginning to hate London and say how unfriendly the people were, and how filthy everything was, and expensive. They neither of them belonged here, and should never have tried living here in the first place: it was time they went back.

'She keeps on at me nowadays, wanting to know when I'm going to get a transfer to Wales.'

'Couldn't that be her way of showing she worries about you? You've been in one or two hairy situations, I daresay?'

Edwards shivered momentarily at the recollection of that dash for the car outside the bank, waiting to be pumped any

131

second full of slugs. But he said: 'No more than anyone else on my relief.'

'But she's not married to anyone else. Isn't it possible she just wants you out of the firing line?'

'Could be,' said Edwards sceptically. 'Stuck behind a whelk stall on Llandudno sea front. Then she'd be really happy.'

Mills sat back and studied him for a long moment. His eyebrows were very dark and bushy, shadowing his eyes. 'Now, hold it a minute. Didn't you just say she wanted you to get a transfer? Not trying to contradict you, but – '

'Yes, all right. Forget about the whelk stall,' Edwards conceded, 'but you know what I mean. She's a small-town girl with small-minded parents, and they all like living in each others' pockets.'

'And you don't like that?'

Edwards thought dourly of how anxious he had been to escape just that very suffocating atmosphere. In coming to London he had been turning his back on boredom, lack of money, lack of freedom. Now he did not want to face creeping back to his home town and in-laws and nodding agreement to every petty little prejudice they uttered.

He said: 'I don't like the idea of being expected to spend the rest of my life slagging off the big city.'

'How long were you here on your own before you got married?'

'About three years.'

'And were you happy?' When there was no reply, Mills suggested: 'The bachelor life in London suits a lot of young coppers. Did it suit you, d'you think – is that what you're missing?'

'Not really. Getting tanked up and talking smut in a loud voice has never been my scene.'

'And since you've been married? Even less one of the lads, perhaps?'

Edwards had to nod to this. 'Being the only married man on the relief, yes.'

Mills had ceased to scribble down any notes. He tapped his

ballpoint throughtfully on the pad. 'What you're basically saying,' he suggested at last, 'is that, one way or another, you've never really fitted in up here?'

Edwards wanted to snap out an indignant denial. Somehow it failed to come.

In the LIO room a floorboard creaked loudly as Chief Inspector Conway put his weight on it. He shifted irritably to one side, distracted from the query he had been following up with Cathy Marshall and Viv Martella.

'Get maintenance to fix that, will you?'

'Sir?'

'That board.' He rammed his heel down to demonstrate.

'Sir.'

'Now, this list of unsolved break-ins they've been pestering us about . . .' He stepped forward to take the sheet of paper she was holding out to him, and the board under his feet dipped and squeaked again.

'It's only started doing that today,' Cathy commented.

'Probably only needs a nail.'

Impatiently Conway stooped and pulled back the edge of the lino to expose the boards underneath. The edges of two of them were slightly raised and loose. Conway prodded one, and it responded with another creak. He got his fingers under the edge, and tugged upwards. The board came free with surprising ease. He stared in. Cathy Marshall, leaning over her desk, gasped. In the space below the two loose boards was the gleam of metal. Conway got his fingers into the plastic webbing and lifted out two four-packs of lager cans.

He turned a malevolent gaze on the two women.

'Not yours by any chance, Martella?'

'Oh no, sir. I only drink gin.'

Conway got to his feet, brushed dust from his knees, and set the cans on Cathy's desk.

'I'm sure everyone in this place knows that alcohol is forbidden on the premises.'

'I'm sure they do, sir.'

'So who do you suppose has started hoarding the stuff? And is there any more of it – lots of little caches, in case the owner gets thirsty at any stage of the day?'

Cathy Marshall groaned inwardly. Conway was a stickler. Once he got his teeth into something, there was no way of loosening them until he had won his battle. It looked as if Sun Hill was due for a fanatical investigation.

Conway confirmed her fears. 'I'm going to sort this one out. Right now.'

He took up the cans of lager and headed out along the corridor. PC Richard Turnham, approaching from the CAD room, glanced down with mild surprise.

'Not yours either, I suppose, Turnham?'

'Sir?'

'These eight cans of lager. Secreted under the collator's lino. No, forget it.' He thrust past Turnham. 'I don't see you as a lager man.' He made his way to the duty inspector's office and dumped the eight offending cans on the desk under Christine Frazer's nose. 'Under the collator's lino,' he said again. 'I'm putting a notice in the canteen inviting the owners to claim.'

'Hardly likely to elicit a response, is it?'

'I just want them to know that *I* know. No alcohol on the premises – they know the rules.'

'If there's any more I expect it'll be removed quite rapidly now.'

'You're dead right it will,' vowed Conway, 'because I'm going to find it.'

'Yes, well, if you'll excuse me, sir' – Frazer obviously did not give the quest quite the same high priority as did Conway – 'I do have a GBH in the charge room.'

She left the office. Conway was about to follow, but an unworthy suspicion crossed his mind. He sidled towards the ancient filing cabinet in the corner of the room, and pulled open the top drawer for a surreptitious glance inside.

Inspector Frazer reappeared in a hurry, snatching up a

folder from her desk. She favoured him with a bland smile. 'I keep a change of underwear in that one, sir.'

Taffy Edwards was not sure he could take much more. If he didn't like talking about himself, still less did he like other people talking about him and asking questions he was reluctant to answer.

'Yes,' he said with an effort, 'I do love my wife, yes.'

'And it's pretty clear she loves you, isn't it?' said Mills gently. 'I mean, that was quite a brave thing to do, following you up to London. From what you say there must have been a lot of parental pressure to stay put.' He paused. 'Maybe she wanted to break away as much as you did. What d'you think?'

Remembering all the eager talk there had been, and the hopes for the future and the long discussions about her mother and father, Edwards had to admit the justice of this. But that all dealt with the hopeful times, when they were setting out. Things had gone sour since then, slowly, almost without him noticing the hows and whys of the gradual build-up.

He managed a nod.

'So is it possible,' Mills went on carefully, 'that the real problem is not so much that Mary wants to go back to Wales, but that *you* want to go back but can't bring yourself to admit it? So you're having to offload the blame on to "the wife".'

Edwards mulled this over. At last he said bitterly: 'Well, it'll be the final proof that Taffy Edwards hides from trouble, won't it?'

Mills' eyebrows rose sharply. 'Any truth in that?'

'No.'

'Well, then. Don't you think it'll show a lot more guts to move out than to stay put, even if you get a lot of stick from your mates? I think if it was me, I'd talk things through with my wife, take a deep breath and go for it.' He waited for a response. When none came, he added: 'Maybe we should meet again and have another chat.'

135

Edwards stood up abruptly. 'No. No, thanks very much. I'm sorry to have taken up your time.'

He could not wait to get out of here, into his car, and away. But when he was seated behind the wheel, ready to go, he realised dismally that he still had to choose a destination. All that talk had still left him with decisions to make on his own. Or, as Mills had suggested, with Mary.

The locker room was empty save for a pile of litter, a billiard cue case propped against one wall, and a cardboard box which on examination proved to contain not lager cans but several pairs of smelly trainers. Conway swore to himself that this was going to be the next purge. The station was a disgrace. The whole place needed a thorough clean-up. For the moment, however, he had other things to do. Closing the door behind him, he stared up suspiciously at the ceiling. One of the tiles seemed to be slightly proud of the others. Taking the cue case, he clambered up on to the bench in the middle of the room and prodded the tile. A few flecks of plaster dropped on his collar and shoulders. Just as he was reaching up to dislodge the tile and explore the ceiling cavity within, the locker room door opened.

PC Turnham studied the scene with polite incredulity.

'Are you following me around, Turnham?'

'No, sir. I've come for my biscuits.'

Turnham went to his locker, opened it, took out a packet of biscuits, carefully locked the cupboard, and went out without a backward glance. Conway waited until he was sure there would be no inquisitive return visit, and then stretched his arm so that he could grope into the opening. There were no cans. Scraping along a beam, though, his fingers encountered a piece of paper. He took it out and turned it to read wording which had been boldly written in capitals with a marker pen.

The message was: SORRY NOT HERE.

Thirteen

The blind man lay staring blankly up at the ceiling. Beside his hospital bed DS Alastair Greig sat with his legs crossed, a notebook on one knee, prompting the injured man gently and without too much pressure. The pain and shock were still too immediate. But so were the memories, and Greig needed to capture them before time could blur them.

'Any idea how many of them, Mr Horsfield?'

'Three men.' It hurt Horsfield to talk, but he was as keen as Greig to get things clear. 'I could hear their voices as they came towards me.'

'Young?'

Horsfield nodded, then winced. After that he kept his head very still, as if not just avoiding pain but thinking very, very carefully so that he could summon up and re-live every little detail.

The three, whoever they were, had been laughing and talking in the distance. Nothing out of the ordinary. Then there was a silence. He had sensed that this was when they saw him. It was followed by a sort of whispering. Then they came a lot closer, until he could tell they were just in front of him. He tapped his way on, suspecting nothing. There was nothing really, except that odd silence, to worry him. They were just standing there. He passed close enough to touch one of them with his stick. He said, 'Excuse me,' and tried to move slightly away.

There was a hand on his arm. One of the young men was asking if he had any money to spare. He told them no. 'Right,' came the rasping voice, 'we'll have this, then.' He felt his stick being tugged away from him, and tried to hold on to it. Then there was a terrific bang in his face, and he fell over. Two of the men were holding him down while the other felt for his wallet. It was crazy. There was only fifteen pounds in it. That didn't please them. Horsfield heard his stick being broken, and they were cursing at him, and he thought they were going to storm off. He lay quite still, waiting for the sound of their footsteps hurrying away. Instead, he got a boot in the ribs, and then another in the head.

After that he had no idea what happened, or how long it was before he heard the police constable's voice.

Greig said quietly: 'Was there anything about the voices you remember? You could differentiate between them?'

'One was a black voice, I think. You know, West Indian.'

'Was he the one who spoke to you directly?'

'No.' Horsfield spoke in an undertone, but kept it very firm. 'The other two were Cockney. It was one of them – a bit of an older one, I'd say – who asked me for the money.'

'Would you recognise that particular voice again?'

'Oh, yes.' There was a slight croak in Horsfield's throat. He hoisted himself awkwardly up in the bed and held out a hand in appeal.

It took a moment for the message to penetrate. Then Greig apologetically poured a glass of water from the carafe on the bedside table and set it carefully in Horsfield's hand. When the glass was empty he replaced it on the table.

'How about smell? Alcohol, maybe?'

'They'd definitely been drinking. Beer, lager . . . not spirits.'

'Did they sound very drunk?'

'Not slurred, no.'

'Aftershave?' Greig suggested.

Instinctively Horsfield shook his head again, and obviously regretted it. 'A stale, unwashed sort of smell,' he said.

'All of them?'

'Yes.' Horsfield brooded for a moment, then added: 'The one that held my shoulders, when I was on the ground . . . he smelt of cars.'

Greig leaned forward, alert. 'Cars?'

'Oil. Like he had engine dirt on his hands.'

Greig began to feel a twinge of optimism. In spite of his injuries Mr Horsfield was proving an admirable witness. Jotting down a few notes, he ventured a question about clothes. It seemed a bit of a flyer, and you could hardly expect a blind man to come out with much in the way of visual description. But Horsfield was game. During the brief struggle when he was trying to keep hold of his cane and grabbing out to keep himself upright, he thought he had scraped his fingers on 'some tee shirt kind of material'. And when he was down, one of them who kicked him was wearing jeans. He was pretty sure of that.

'Anything else?'

'No. Sorry. That's about it.'

'Not to worry,' said Greig reassuringly. He leaned over the bed and studied the bruised face. 'It looks like the guy who punched you could have been wearing a ring.'

Horsfield almost managed a smile. 'Yes, he was. Hadn't thought of that. Yes, I felt it as he was trying to pull my stick away. Before he let go and hit me.' He pondered again. Greig, not wanting to interrupt, held his breath. 'On his right hand,' said Horsfield at last.

Jubilantly Greig wrote it down. 'What did it feel like? A signet ring?'

'Quite big, yes. Lumpy.'

'Great.' Greig went on writing. 'That's great, Mr Horsfield.'

It was enough for one session. The victim had struggled gallantly on, but was showing signs of exhaustion. Greig snapped his notebook shut and left. His first port of call at Sun Hill had to be the LIO room. It seemed another good omen, when he got there, that Norika Datta was in the room talking to Cathy Marshall. It could all save time.

'Obviously our friends approached Mr Horsfield from the direction of Webley Road,' Greig summed up. 'So they must have passed within yards of that car park while you were there, Norika. You didn't hear anything?'

'Could have been while we were on our way to the top.'

'Looking down from the top, then. See anything at all?'

'Sorry, no.'

'And the kids who found him saw no one either?'

'No.'

Greig sighed, and thought for a minute. 'Pubs in the vicinity?'

On this territory at least Norika was knowledgeable. 'The nearest one's the *Belmont Arms*. Then there's the *Queen's Head*.'

'And the *Blackbird*?' Cathy contributed.

'No.' Norika was quite firm. 'That's in the wrong direction if they came from Webley Road.'

'So we're possibly looking for three guys who used the *Belmont Arms* or the *Queen's Head* at lunchtime.'

It was Cathy's turn to be firm. 'The *Queen's Head*'s been yuppified. If we're talking real slag it's more likely to be the *Belmont*.'

There was little doubt that they were talking real slag. And Greig was becoming increasingly sure that this would have been a tightly knit little group. You might lay into a copper or two with guys you had just met in the pub, but you didn't beat up blind people. There had to be a real rapport for that. He would have taken a bet that those three knocked around together a lot. Perhaps this was a line to which the collator might turn her attention.

Meanwhile WPC Datta could get back out of doors and start looking.

'Enquiries *Belmont Arms* and adjacent area,' said Greig. 'I'll clear it with Inspector Frazer. Did anyone see three young men, one black, two white. One wearing jeans and a tee-shirt. One with oily hands. One with a large signet ring.'

'But where'd you get all this?' demanded Norika. 'The victim was blind, we know that.'

'He's just more observant than a lot of people who can see.'

Norika Datta took this personally. 'Right, sergeant.'

She went off to collect Quinnan and resume their patrol.

Cathy Marshall eyed DS Greig with cool disfavour. 'That wasn't very nice.'

'Mm? Oh, sorry. Wasn't thinking. Just that you get a case where you expect nothing and then suddenly you've got a chance . . .'

He waited in mute appeal. She said: 'And I suppose you expect me to reel off all the muggers known to wear signet rings.'

'It'd be a start.'

Cathy turned resignedly towards her filing cabinets. 'I'll see what I can do.'

Quinnan was combing his hair at the washroom mirror when Richard Turnham came in, glancing at himself fleetingly in the glass and looking a trifle smug.

'Time for a cup of tea, Rich?'

'Er, thanks, no. Not right now.' Turnham held it for a moment, then could not resist. 'Just been having a china cup job, actually. With the chief super.'

'Ah. Still the blue-eyed boy, then?'

'Brownlow's seen *you*, I suppose? Welcome to the new boy, and so on.'

'Not yet,' said Quinnan wryly.

'Oh. Well.'

'Get on all right with him, do you?'

'Why not?'

'Why not, indeed. No temptations, anyway. I hear his wife's a bit of an old dog.'

Turnham slammed round against the washroom door, pressing it shut. He raised a clenched fist.

'Come off it, only a joke,' Quinnan protested.

'Let's just keep that private, shall we?'

'I'd never tell a soul. Come on, Rich, we're mates. Aren't we?'

There was a heave against the door from the other side. Turnham stood back to allow Tony Stamp in.

'Oh, you're here, Dave. Datta's out there raring to go.'

'Like I said, they just can't wait to get at me.'

Dave Quinnan went out to resume the patrol, but even as

141

they were leaving the station he said decisively: 'No more car parks, right?'

She made no direct answer but filled him in on the new instructions. They made straight for the *Belmont Arms*, and within five minutes knew there would be no joy there. Such daylight as managed to filter through the grimy windows did so only with difficulty, and the feeble bulbs over the bar would make the identifications of correct change a major gamble. The landlord either had no regular customers at all, or no brain cells attuned to recognising them when and if they appeared. He would not have remembered if he had served Dolly Parton topless: except that there would have been nowhere to put the glass.

'You're still sulking,' Quinnan accused Datta as they set off along the cracked stones of the pavement.

'No, I'm not.'

'You are. I can tell by the way you keep tripping over your bottom lip.'

Before she could reply, Melvin's voice in her radio began reporting a suspected theft at Morgan's the Jeweller's in Pring Street. Still a newcomer to the area, Quinnan raised an enquiring eyebrow. Pring Street was in fact just round the corner. Norika Datta felt immediately enlivened, and within seconds was on her way, hurrying him along and almost baring her teeth in her eagerness to get to grips with some real solid trouble.

The shop had a shabby frontage, tucked into a narrow space between a cycle repair shop and a greengrocer's. It was difficult to see in through the steel mesh over the window, and for a moment the door would not open. Then the latch buzzed and they were admitted to find the place a whole lot brighter inside. A few strategically placed lights struck colour and silvery sparks from rings and jewels in display cases.

A small tableau seemed to have frozen into position by the glass counter. A middle-aged man and a young woman assistant stood behind it. In front of it was a young man in a

142

loose blue plastic jacket and brown slacks, trying to look casual and patient but mildly indignant at the same time.

'Right, then,' he said as the police officers came into the shop, 'let's get it over with. Then maybe you'll be satisfied.'

Quinnan looked at the man behind the counter. 'Are you the proprietor, sir?'

'That's me. George Morgan. This man has stolen a diamond stud.'

'I've stolen nothing.'

'He comes into the shop and asks to see a tray of studs from the window.' Morgan indicated a tray on the counter between them. 'I look away for a split second. When I look back, one of the studs is gone.'

Quinnan leaned over the tray. 'There seem to be several gone.'

'The others have been sold. But not that one. That space was *not* empty before he got his hands on it.'

A police car drew up outside the door. The latch buzzed again, to admit PC Tony Stamp in answer to Melvin's radio call.

'What's the problem?'

Morgan groaned. To save him the trouble of going through it again, Quinnan hastily summarised the situation. Norika Datta crouched to edge her way across the floor around their feet, examining every inch of the carpet.

'Marjorie's already done that,' said Morgan impatiently. 'I tell you, *he's* got it.'

Quinnan looked at the young man, who maintained a picture of injured innocence, pained but patient.

'I suppose you want to strip search me?'

'I don't think that'll be necessary, Mr . . .?'

'Beck.'

'Perhaps you wouldn't mind turning out your pockets, Mr Beck. Seems the quickest way of settling the argument.'

Beck shrugged, and went methodically through his pockets, emptying them with calculated slowness. The diary, tube of

143

cough sweets, cigarette packet and lighter made an unremarkable centrepiece to some scraps of paper and a blurred mauve till receipt for something or other. Stamp courteously asked him to raise his arms, and swiftly frisked him.

'I'll have to make a note of your name and address, sir. All searches have to be recorded.'

'No problem.' Beck began replacing the contents of his pockets. He stared across the counter at the proprietor. 'Just be grateful I don't sue you.'

'If you'd just come out to the car, I'll get my log sheet.'

Stamp was opening the door and standing politely aside when Quinnan, glancing across the street through the widening gap, said abruptly:

'Would that be your girlfriend over the way, Mr Beck?'

Beck tensed, then managed a blank look. 'Huh?'

A young woman staring with apparently rapt concentration into a window on the far side of the street took a quick glance round, then resumed her contemplation. Stamp edged across the open doorway, puzzled but now blocking Beck's exit rather than holding the door open for him.

Quinnan turned back to the counter and ran a finger slowly under its metal rim. He smiled. Morgan watched as a small diamond stud was brought out, pressed into a piece of chewing-gum.

'Coming in for this later, was she?' said Quinnan affably.

'I don't know what you're – '

'Must be your chewing-gum, sir. It's still soft.'

Stamp and Datta exchanged nods of unabashed admiration, and beamed at Dave Quinnan. Pretty good, it had to be admitted, for his first day out on the manor.

Stamp was a little less pleased when within a short space of time, as he put it with a hint of sour grapes on his tongue, 'Dempsey and Makepeace struck again', all in the same day and on the same tour of duty.

It happened within ten minutes of the two of them setting out in the early evening to round off their tour of duty on foot patrol. Norika Datta was pointing out various local sites and potential trouble spots, and Dave Quinnan was nodding with a certain loftiness. After his spell of smart deduction, he was not exactly enamoured of drab routine.

'The house on the end there,' Datta persevered, 'is a new bail hostel.'

'Give you any problems?'

'Not as many as some people thought it would.'

He shrugged disdainfully. 'Had a children's home on my last ground. Absolutely outrageous. If we had one call a week we had twenty. Drugs, knives, soliciting . . . and that was just the staff. As for what went on behind the . . .'

His voice trailed away as he realised that Datta was paying no attention. She had slowed her pace and was staring across the road. A man carrying a plastic shopping bag was coming down the outer steps from an upper level to the ground floor of the multi-storey car park. Datta's hand on Quinnan's arm brought them to a halt.

'That's him,' she breathed.

'Who?'

'The car con-man.'

'Eh?' Quinnan watched the man disappear into the shadows of the ground floor. 'Can't say I noticed any label.'

Datta was already leading the way across the road. He followed her silently across the concrete floor as the man turned into one of the wide bays. They moved behind a concrete pillar as he continued his saunter along the line of parked cars. He could have been any ordinary driver slowly making his way to his own vehicle from the nearby shopping precinct; only it was funny to come down from a higher level to this lower one if his car had been here all along. Getting forgetful about where he had left it?

Datta's suspect stopped beside a blue Fiat, tentatively fingered the bonnet, and had a hurried look round. Somewhere on the far side a car accelerated, slowed for the exit, and whined away into the distance. The man produced a thin screwdriver blade from his bag, and inserted it under the car bonnet. After two careful slides to one side and another he leaned over it, pushed slightly harder, and sprang the catch.

By the time Datta and Quinnan approached, the bonnet was propped open and the man's head was inside it.

Datta glanced at Quinnan. Gallantly he waved her to proceed.

Pleasantly she said: 'Is this your car, sir?'

The man stood up. He tried to smile and was obviously hunting for plausible words. But then he stared full into Norika Datta's face, and realisation dawned.

She tugged her radio closer to her lips and called for a car to pick up the con-man and themselves. It seemed to make everything even more agreeably tidy that the nearest driver should again be Tony Stamp. They arrived at Sun Hill in a mood of some euphoria. Sergeant Penny greeted them with an appreciative smile. He started to congratulate Quinnan, who at once said: 'Norika's collar, this one, sarge. Nothing to do with me.'

Perhaps all this sweetness and light were growing too sickening for Penny's taste. He noticed a car parked close by his left foot, and scowled at it. 'Just a minute. What's your car doing in the yard, Norika?'

'Sorry, sarge, I couldn't find a space outside and I was late.'

'So you were. But it shouldn't still be there. Book your prisoner in and get it shifted.'

Stamp and Penny accompanied the prisoner into the station. Dave Quinnan looked at Norika's car, pursed his lips knowingly, and patted the bonnet.

'Starts first time, does it?'

She tried not to look sheepish.

It was turning out to be quite a productive day at Sun Hill. Complacency was not one of Cathy Marshall's vices, but today, like some of the others, she felt she could be reasonably proud of her deductive faculties. It was in hopeful mood that she made her way from the LIO room to the CID office, notebook at the ready. Alastair Greig and Tosh Lines were drinking coffee and appeared to have all the time in the world. She had news which ought to waken them out of their somnolence.

'Your three musketeers. I've spoken to as many beat officers as I can, and they're not all as unobservant as you seem to think.'

Greig raised a hand in a gesture of apology. Before he could make any excuses Cathy went on. It appeared in fact that there were no less than three groups of possibles roaming the manor. Not a pleasant prospect for law-abiding citizens. But not many of these groups were known to the collator in a CRO sense, so she had checked back through prisoners' property records of those who were, and had come up with a name which might merit some attention.

Stephen Robert Charlesworth had had a signet ring when he was arrested in July 1988 for a breach of the peace. He also had a younger brother, Clifford, and both of them lived on the notorious Pilbeam Estate, where they spent a good deal of their time creating a nuisance by cannibalising dumped motor cars in a messy and noisy manner. 'With their friend Roy Wilkes, IC3,' she added significantly. That rang a bell with Tosh Lines. 'And we have Stephen's fingerprints on record,' Cathy concluded, 'so if you can match them up with those on the white stick, you're home and dry.'

Lines blinked, hearing further bells, and shook himself fully awake. Half his mind had been drifting dismally over the uproar at home when the television had been repossessed because of a little matter of defaulting payments, and some remarks about a need for some new shoes if the kids were not to dance barefoot along the street to school.

'The stick has been dusted, presumably?' said Cathie.

Greig was on his feet, reaching for the plastic bag with fragments of white stick. It would take until the morning to get a reliable print match, but he did not intend to wait. There ought to be enough to pull the three men in if tackled in the right way. Only it had better be soon: if word got round they

147

would be on their bikes in minutes. He wanted half a dozen uniformed men – and, preferably, a dog.

Inspector Frazer jibbed at the number and at the panic. Resources were tightly stretched, and two men were down with a particularly venomous virus. Finally she agreed to Garfield heading for the scene in his panda, and others being wheeled in to meet him. Garfield, involved in the Charlesworth arrest last year, knew every way into that council estate and every way the quarry might try to get out.

Greig and Lines drove to a rendezvous well back from the eastern fringe of the estate. Garfield had already picked up Melvin and Turnham. On the far side of the estate the dog handler would be waiting to close in with Stamp and two other PCs. They had better be there. Greig wanted this over and done with, neatly, all at one go – not some chase that dragged out over the months, until the original crime had blurred in everyone's memory save that of Mr Horsfield.

He glanced at Garfield.

'Just follow the noise,' said Garfield knowledgeably.

He and the detective sergeant led the way. The music grew louder as they went, accompanied by the harsh, repeated revving of a car engine. Round a corner they came on what had been meant as a residents' parking area but had degenerated into a virtual breaker's yard. A couple of burnt-out, wheel-less hulks were propped up on bricks, though it was impossible to see what function they could ever fulfil again. Doors and a couple of back seats had been dumped to one side. In the middle of it a young man was working inside a car which still had its doors and wheels intact, one of them continuing to rev the engine. Someone was sprawled underneath. Set on an oil drum, a ghetto blaster pumped out noise at full volume.

Greig paused. To his relief Stamp's area car cruised quietly into view on the far side of the trodden grass beyond the parking area. A dog handler eased an Alsatian out of the boot. They waited for a signal.

The signal was abrupt and impressive. Greig simply

stepped forward and turned off the ghetto blaster. The car engine whined down from its hysterical top note, and there was an eerie silence.

'Hey, leave it off . . .'

The young man at the wheel of the car lurched out and straightened up aggressively.

Greig said calmly: 'Stephen Charlesworth?'

Charlesworth looked wonderingly at the line of policemen strolling into an ever-tightening arc before him. A quick glance back over his shoulder, and they waited for him to make a dash for it. The dog raised its head. Charlesworth's pale, ferrety little face went paler. But he stayed where he was as Garfield and Melvin edged in on either side, and Tosh Lines indicated that the man under the car should haul himself out before he got hauled out.

Chief Inspector Conway added stiff congratulations to those showering over the heads of the incoming team, but his face was grim and basically unresponsive. His mind was elsewhere. The trouble was, he could not be sure where this elsewhere might be.

He looked cautiously into the cupboard beside the canteen door, but all that happened was that a broom toppled forward and narrowly missed his nose. Slamming the door, he went on his way. Upstairs there was a lot of activity. It would have to wait until later. Downstairs, the door from the yard had ceased swinging to and fro and the prisoners were being lined up for the charge room, while Sergeant Peters allocated the cell numbers in readiness. Conway realised he had not so far looked into the property store. It seemed a natural place to hide things. He glanced back, slid in through the door and ran one hand along the nearest rack. All it acquired was a coating of dust. There was going to be a right roistering about this mess before he was finished.

He came to a cupboard at the end, and carefully opened the door, bracing himself for another attack from a broom.

Pinned inside the door was a note: NICE TRY BUT NO.

Fourteen

Chief Inspector Conway had two things on his mind as he set about briefing afternoon parade. One had been provoked by a directive floating down from far above. The other was a matter of personal provocation. The Sun Hill contingent could make what they liked of the balance between the two, but so far as he was concerned they were going to suffer from the way he interpreted both aspects.

He started with a formal address, echoing official guidelines about the whole question of image. It was the real buzz word nowadays: image. The Force's image of itself, the public's image of the Force. The way policemen and policewomen dressed, the way they spoke to people. Politeness and compassion were in, just as in the textbooks and sentimental films of the old days. Abrasiveness and lack of courtesy were out. To emphasise this he glared at random, and provoked an alarmed, half-guilty start from PC Tony Stamp.

With this directive out of the way, Conway switched to what had been bothering him these last few days.

'The way we live in this station,' he grated, 'is a disgrace. That rat's nest you call a locker room. Rubbish stuffed away – *hidden* away – God knows where. Everywhere. And don't think I won't find it eventually,' he added obscurely, looking round in the hope of a revealing snigger or twitch of a facial muscle. 'Take a leaf from WPC Marshall. A place for everything and everything in its place.'

Cathy Marshall looked as if she could well have done without such a compliment from such a source.

Conway drew himself up for a final peroration. 'Let's start being aware of what we're trying to *do* and *be* and how we match up to what the world outside expects. Little things mean a lot, so let's all make that little extra effort . . .' He was distracted by WPC Martella's apparent lack of interest as she craned her neck back over her shoulder and twitched her left leg. 'What's the matter, Martella?'

'Sorry, sir. I've got a ladder in my tights.'

There seemed little point in going on with any expectation of dutiful attention. Brusquely, Conway rounded off: 'Efficient service with a smile. That's what Joe Public wants. And that's what I want, too. Carry on.'

As he stumped out of the door he was caught up by PC Tim Able. 'Uh, sir . . .' Conway reluctantly slackened to hear whatever bleat this might be. He was in no mood for moans from the ranks. 'I was wondering,' said Able fervently. 'I'm on three beat this afternoon, and I'm wondering if it would be okay to take out a push-bike. I mean, I was talking to a couple of the guys on early turn and they reckon they're really the business, push-bikes – especially in the rush hour.'

Conway summoned up several tart rejoinde s, ~nd suddenly found himself taken by the notion. 'Good image,' he agreed. 'Yes, sure. Bobby on bike. Human, accessible.' But he hedged his bets: 'Just clear it with Inspector Frazer.'

'Yes, sir.'

Able went off looking pleased with himself before there was anything all that substantial to feel pleased about.

Viv Martella, still dragging her leg and looking down reproachfully at the ladder, made the mistake of crossing Conway's path.

'Ah. Martella. You won't mind doing surgery this afternoon, will you?'

'Surgery, sir? I mean, I'm only a home beat officer, not a home help or – '

'Consultation,' said Conway acidly. 'At Pilbeam Estate. You know the ground well enough, and it's only a couple of hours. Now Community Liaison has established a rapport, I'd hate to cancel just because Hollis is off colour this week.'

Martella's views on the colour of Reg Hollis, on or off, were

151

explicit in her expression without ever actually contravening any race relations laws.

'It's a long way, sir. Right on the far side of my patch.'

'Get someone to give you a lift. Stamp and Ackland should be leaving any minute.'

There was no way out of it. Viv Martella went out to the yard as Stamp was about to set off. Ahead of them, Tim Able was wheeling a bike from the shed.

Stamp stared and wound down his window. 'You're never going out on that? In broad daylight?'

Able displayed his complete confidence by giving one push, swinging his leg across the bar, and coasting smoothly towards the gates.

'Remember, then,' Stamp called after him. 'No wheelies in the play park. Oh, and if we're up against anything a bit quick I'll give you a shout.'

Martella tapped on the window to indicate that she needed a lift. Stamp groaned. 'Don't like female operators in my vehicle. Two at one go is pushing it a bit.'

'Conway's orders.'

'If you were on a bike,' said June Ackland sweetly, 'he couldn't have asked.'

'Hm. *Him*.' As they moved away, Stamp said derisively: 'What did you make of that rubbish back there? Just a load of PR squit.'

'Being nice?' said Ackland.

'We're not paid to be nice.'

'Just as well. You wouldn't earn much.'

'We're paid to nick villains. Do more of that, and Joe Public'll be perfectly happy whether you tell him to have a nice day or not.'

'Tell you what. I'll do the smiling, you concentrate on driving. It'll save you time trying to do two things at once.'

Stamp glowered but did not summon up any retort. They covered a couple of miles in silence, and then he waved at two cars keeping a decorous pace ahead. 'Lovely, isn't it, the way they all drive so impeccably when they see a police motor.'

'Gives you a feeling of power, does it, Tony?'

He grinned. Then his mind went back to the briefing. 'And what about all those hints of Conway's? About stuff hidden away?'

'I didn't get that,' Martella confessed.

'Just following up that nudge-nudge thing he stuck on the canteen noticeboard inviting someone to claim their illicit booze. Now he thinks every inch of the panelling is lousy with lager.'

'Any minute now we'll have a breathalyser on every parade.'

'It's gotta be the night shift, hasn't it?'

'Which night shift?' asked Ackland. 'We're all on nights one week in three, and I haven't seen any booze around.'

'Maybe you're not playing it clever enough. The right sort of nod and wink, and a bit of the you-know-what, and then someone'd offer you some.'

'I'll stick to buying my own, I think.'

As if to throw the two women off balance, Stamp accelerated, raced past the two cars, and swung at a tight angle into a side street and down to the edge of the Pilbeam Estate, scene of a recent bit of policing of the kind he approved of. He stopped with a jolt and reached back to open the passenger door.

'Here you are, my love. Three quid on the clock.'

'The community hall's round the back,' Martella protested.

'Then you'll enjoy the walk, won't you?'

Stiffly she got out, slammed the door, and set off along the slimy path between its patches of hard-trodden, rubbish-strewn grass.

PC Tim Able pedalled contentedly along. It was a nicer sensation than he had remembered. Quite some time since he had cycled out down the suburban lanes behind his school, finding a different way home or a different place to explore at

153

weekends. He had joined the Force with a burning ambition to get into one of the cars. Now he felt there were perfectly simple, ordinary sensations he had been missing. A couple of kids waved to him. He waved back, wobbled, and tried the brakes as he approached some untidy parking along the pavement of the shopping parade.

The back of a middle-aged, blue Cortina estate jutted out at an angle, as if the driver had shoved it into the gap in a hurry. A woman's elbow rested on the driver's door. Slowing, Able glanced idly at the rear number plate, smeared with grime but legible enough to strike a vague chord. He slowed past the car, checked the road was clear, and swung round full circle to have a look at the front.

The woman was getting out. She looked at him as he dismounted, and started to walk away briskly.

'Excuse me, madam.' As her pace quickened, Able trundled his bike out into the road and then cut across to intercept her. He raised his voice. 'Excuse me, madam.'

She could either turn or run. He looked quickly round to see where he could prop his bike if he had to give chase along the pavement.

She decided to wait for him.

He said with a politeness which Conway would surely have commended: 'Is this your car, madam?'

'Er, no. No. I just noticed the lights were on.' She had a hoarse voice, perhaps the result of too much gin and too many cigarettes. She might have been in her late twenties, but her face was lined as if she had twisted it too vehemently, too often, in too many rows. 'Door wasn't locked, so I got in and turned them off.'

'That was very good of you. It's definitely not yours?'

'No, I've told you.'

'Could you wait just a minute, please.' He reached for his radio.

'Why? I haven't done nothing.'

'Sierra Oscar from 139,' said Able, 'receiving? Over.'

'Go ahead, 139,' said Richard Turnham's voice.

154

'I've got a blue Cortina estate, registration . . .' He craned his neck and carefully recited: 'DSR 584T. Could you check it against details of the vehicle involved in the wages snatch yesterday in Chater Street.'

'Will do.'

'And I might need some transport, please.'

The woman was looking nervously from side to side as a small crowd began to gather. 'Look, it's not my car. I've never seen it before.'

Transport was quick to arrive. Stamp and Ackland could have been no further than a street away. As the car pulled in behind Able's bike, Stamp leaned out of the window. 'Call for assistance, Tim? What's the matter – got a puncture?'

'Just a collar,' said Able. 'Division of labour, see? I do the catching, you ferry them back to the nick.'

He watched them shepherd the unwilling yet unresisting woman into the car, and happily got on his bike again.

Stamp and Ackland delivered their charge to Sun Hill, where she was booked in as Mrs Natalie Rickard, by now beginning to get more voluble and swearing that someone was going to be done for this, mark her flaming words.

There was an air of festivity in the canteen. Business today seemed brisk and fruitful. Conway's notice on the canteen board asking for the owner of four cans of lager to come forward and claim them might have contained a veiled threat, but its main effect was to produce incredulous laughter and a lot of speculation about the phantom can-carrier. June Ackland edged her way through the cheerful crowd towards the serving hatch, where Stamp was already holding forth to Turnham about the afternoon's events so far.

'Point being that when you're driving an area car you depend on your operator being on the ball, don't you. You're watching the road, your operator's supposed to be looking for work.' Stamp grunted. 'Get a stumer beside you, and you've got no chance.'

Ackland was at his shoulder. 'I saw this, though, didn't I?' She held a key in front of his nose. 'You didn't. Looks like a

Cortina ignition key. Our Mrs Rickard had stuffed it down our back seat.'

Stamp tried to shrug it off as he reached for a cup of tea. Before he could find himself a chair far enough from June Ackland, PC Martin had intercepted him. 'All set, Tony?'

'Eh? What you on about?'

'Didn't Frazer tell you? Me and Sam'll be coming out with you after your break.'

'Sam?'

'Me dog.'

Stamp stared blankly. Clearly it was not his day. Without another word to Martin he stormed off in search of Inspector Frazer to protest that mangy Alsatians were not supposed to travel in his sort of motor. Dog handlers had vans for their dogs, and that was the way it ought to be. Christine Frazer smiled tolerantly, and explained that this was yet another experiment in which Sun Hill was expected to co-operate. It had been a great success in other divisions. Instead of sitting in their vans waiting for a call, the handlers took spells travelling in an area car so they could be first on the scene should an incident occur.

'You like being first on the scene, don't you?' she said amiably.

'Of course I do, ma'am, but – '

'Then you'll be glad to have a dog with you. Unless you'd rather spend the rest of your shift on foot?'

'No, ma'am.'

'Well, then.' The inspector waved dismissively. 'Off you go and make friends with Sam.'

Sourly Stamp plodded out to the yard. The hatchback of the car was already up, and Martin was encouraging his Alsatian to jump in. June Ackland smiled admiringly at the animal just as Tim Able pedalled across the yard. She nodded at Stamp.

'Can't take a dog on a bike, either.'

Without a word Stamp got into the driver's seat and waited for Martin to climb in beside him.

'Just one thing,' said Martin confidentially. 'I'd open all the windows if I were you. He's had a bit of a tummy upset. Got bad breath. At both ends.'

How much worse could it get? Stamp wound down his window and headed out into the great, wide, wicked world with a lot less enthusiasm than usual.

In the interview room the tape recorder began to spin, and DS Greig opened his notebook.

'You've been cautioned, Natalie, and you know why you're here.'

'For saving a guy's battery, apparently.'

Greig shook his head sadly and began to intone the drab facts of the case. At nine forty-five the previous morning, two men had snatched a briefcase containing £2,400 from a service station manager in Chater Street while he was on his way to the bank. Shortly afterwards a witness saw a blue Cortina estate, registration DSR 584T, parked in Parview Road with its rear door open. Two men, one carrying a briefcase, jumped in and the car drove off. The driver was a woman.

'And you still deny it was you?'

'Yes,' said Mrs Rickard.

'When you were arrested' – Greig glanced at his notes – 'you were found to be in possession of £475. Can you explain where the money came from?'

'It's me savings.'

'You carry your savings around with you?'

'I was on me way to buy a new sofa.'

'So you'd drawn the money from your bank or building society account?'

'No. I keep it under me bed. Always have done.'

Greig took the ignition key from his pocket and put it on the table between them. 'This fits the blue Cortina.'

'So?'

'It was found where you'd been sitting in the police car.'

'I can't help that, can I?'

'You wouldn't have been trying to hide it there?'

'I've never seen it before.'

'And if your fingerprints are found on it?'

She stared defiantly back at him. 'In that case you made me pick it up, didn't you?'

'Natalie,' said Greig patiently, 'the car is yours. It's been involved in a robbery. Unless you start to co-operate you're looking at a prison sentence of maybe two years. Who are the two men you drove for?'

'I didn't drive for nobody,' said Mrs Rickard doggedly.

She was not going to crack, he could see that. One very stupid woman. Or a very loyal one.

The community hall might at various times be echoing with games or arguments or discos or public lectures – for all the impression such things made on the population of the estate. At this moment the only sound was that of a wheezing woman in a grubby overall sweeping up gluey bits of cardboard and paper. She did not appear to be enjoying her job. Martella was certainly not enjoying hers. She had explained that she was here for the surgery, and then had to explain all over again that she did not mean the surgery which Dr Shah had once conducted but which had since been shifted to the Health Centre. The cleaner snorted and seemed to have no idea what else she could be talking about. At last it began to seep through to her consciousness that the policewoman was talking about police consultation, 'In case people on the estate have got any problems.'

This produced a response. 'I've got a problem all right. The play group. S'posed to clear up after themselves, and look . . . just *look* at it. Well, it's going on me docket. I'm not their unpaid slave.'

Martella decided it would be safer to stay up at the far end of the hall, helping herself to a card table and chair, until the cleaner had finished. When the woman did eventually leave, the whole place seemed even more hollowly resonant. The chore had struck her from the start as a dull one. Now it looked an out-and-out waste of time.

She reached for her radio. 'Sierra Oscar from 227, receiving? Over.'

'Receiving, 227.'

'Are you sure this surgery's not a wind-up? I've been here since God knows when, and there hasn't been a soul wanting to confide in me.'

'Cheer up, Vivien,' said Turnham brightly. 'They also serve who only stand and wait.'

Yes, she thought, but they don't half get bored doing it. She got up. It was not a particularly cold day, but in here the chill seemed to come out of the floor if you just sat around. She ambled aimlessly towards the swing doors at the end of the hall, just as they began to creak open.

Three small children peered round at her. Glad of contact with anyone at all, Martella smiled a welcome.

One of them stared back, leaned a fraction further in, and lobbed an empty soft drink can at her feet. It bounced noisily across the floor as the doors shut again and footsteps went scuttling away.

Martella went back to her card table.

After another long spell of nothingness, she made up her mind. She had sat here and stood here and paced up and down here for a good part of the statutory time decreed by Conway, and now she was ready to quit. She folded the card table and made a move to restack her chair when she became aware that a woman had come timidly into the hall behind her, not making a sound.

'I heard you were here. Sheila told me. You know, the cleaner.'

'Oh.' Martella waited. After a few moments she said encouragingly: 'What's your problem?'

The woman settled herself on the chair Martella had been about to move, and clasped her hands in her lap. 'It's Derek,' she said. 'Me husband. He's gone.'

Martella was reasonably sure that her task was not meant to include marriage guidance council. 'I'm sorry to hear that, Mrs . . . er . . . ?'

159

'Stanley.'

'Well, Mrs Stanley, I'm sorry your husband has left you, but it's not really my – '

'No,' said Mrs Stanley, quiet but obviously determined to get her story out. 'Not that. He's gone to do a job. I know he has. And I don't want him to do any more jobs. He's getting too old for it, and so am I.'

Martella thought of reaching for another chair, but sensed that it might disturb Mrs Stanley's train of thought – or her fumbling confession. She crouched in front of the crumpled, uncertain woman. 'When you say a job,' she coaxed, 'what sort of job?'

'A thieving job.' Mrs Stanley was quite matter-of-fact. 'He's never had any other kind, has he?'

Taken aback, Martella ventured: 'I see. I mean . . . well, when did he go? *Where* did he go?'

'Off about ten minutes since. His nephew's got a van. They're going to do the builders' merchant in Ryton Road.' Mrs Stanley sat back, the weight off her chest. Then she looked concerned. 'Well, what's the matter? Why aren't you . . . well . . . sounding the alarm?'

Martella shifted awkwardly. 'Yes, right. Well. It's just that I almost wish you hadn't told me, love. I wouldn't want people round her to think I'm here to be grassed to. I'm not here for that. I'm here to help.'

Mrs Stanley did not blanch. 'You'll be helping Derek if you nick him,' she said resolutely. 'Silly old fool. Bring him to his senses, and that nephew of his.'

Viv Martella looked at the woman's defeated face; and thought of possible consequences if her husband ever found out who had shopped him; and thought of the dismal consequences if somebody failed to shop him. It was a perverse kind of loyalty, this: but she saw in Mrs Stanley's grey, defeated face the truth of that loyalty. There was no question of marital spite in this.

She dipped her head over her radio.

The message hit Stamp's car just as he was raising certain

queries about animal diet. The dog-handler, Martin, was quite unperturbed. 'He's vegetarian, is our Sam.'

'That means he only bites villains in green trousers?'

'All units from Sierra Oscar.' Turnham's voice broke into their idle chat. 'Information received of possible burglary in progress at Fordham's, the builders' merchants in Ryton Road.'

Stamp shuddered up from his depressive state into one of go-out-and-get-'em. Beside him, June Ackland was galvanised into leaning forward, rapping out the instructions to turn left, then right, and down Gravinner Way. 'Three minutes,' she breathed, 'and we'll be there.'

Stamp was showing that in spite of all the bravado he was a brilliant driver. The siren was on, hooting its screech through the traffic which willingly or clumsily pulled in to make way for it. The dog in the back panted encouragement, as if it wanted to be out of this cramped space and back in business.

June Ackland, looking back over her shoulder, said apprehensively: 'Is he all right?'

'Loves it,' Martin assured her.

They overshot the entry to the street, reversed with a shriek of tyres, and swung down to a standstill outside the open gates of a builders' merchants' yard. Timber was piled high above the level of the outer wall. Within the gates was a decrepit truck loaded with indistinguishable materials, and propped against it a very distinguishable, identifiable push-bike. Tim Able was holding a flabby fifty-year-old man against the edge of the truck. As Stamp and Ackland approached he shouted over his shoulder: 'There's another one somewhere.'

They split up and began to search around the stacks of brick, timber, and miscellaneous junk. In the background they were aware of the sudden excited barking of the Alsatian. Stamp headed in the direction of the noise, only to find himself thumped hideously across the midriff by a length of plank. He collapsed as his attacker, a youngster of about twenty, tossed the wood aside and made a bolt for the fence at the end of the yard. Before he could reach it there was a jubilant snarl, and Martin's dog was launching himself over a pyramid of cardboard boxes. The youth swerved back, leaping over the crumpled figure of Stamp; but the dog was faster, and down went the young man as Martin and Ackland closed in on him.

Stamp, breathlessly tottering to his feet, discovered that close to those feet was the triumphant Tim Able's bicycle. Still gasping for breath, he summoned up the energy to kick it.

Somewhere out in the distance, trudging her way back towards Sun Hill, Viv Martella was wondering whether she had done the right thing.

Chief Inspector Derek Conway was almost at the end of his tether. As a first-rate police officer, he knew what he was after; he could sus out the basic pattern of the villainy now prevailing throughout Sun Hill; and he was sure that all he needed was a sudden intuitive breakthrough. It had worked in a score of criminal cases. Here on his own territory it could hardly fail to be resolved. No grotty little group of subordinates was going to get away with taking the mickey out of him like this.

At the end of what had been a successful afternoon for almost everybody else, he was still in the LIO room systematically ticking off rooms on a layout plan of the entire station. Inspector Frazer, coming through with the cheerful look of one who was glad to shed the cares of the day, looked at his jottings.

'No home to go to, sir?'

'D'you know what, Christine? I've been overlooking the obvious.'

'That's not like you, sir,' she said drily on her way out.

The irony made no impression on Conway. He was already hooked by his splendid inspiration. No further seconds should be wasted. He strode off towards the custody area as Sergeant Peters emerged.

'You busy, Alec?'

Taken off guard, Peters hummed and hawed. 'I . . . er . . . well, sir, I'm on my break. Just off to get my sandwiches.'

'I'll come with you.'

Peters was dumbfounded. 'Eh? I mean, it's only a few bits of . . . I mean, I don't think you'd be all that keen, sort of.'

'In your locker, are they?'

By now Peters was totally fazed. 'I hope so,' he bleated.

Conway waved him onwards with grim, lethal courtesy. Peters led the way towards the sergeants' locker room, glancing back every few seconds to try and size up the situation. By the time they arrived at his locker he was none the wiser.

'Well, go on.' Conway stood above him. 'Open it.'

'Look, sir, what's all this about?'

'Open it.'

Peters put in the key and opened his locker. He had no need to open the door. It sprang out of its own accord to release a shoal of lager cans, clattering in all directions across the floor. He stared, aghast.

Conway was beaming. His sleuthing had at last paid off.

'I've been fitted up,' Peters croaked. He looked for some sympathy, some understanding, in Conway's gloating face. 'I deny all knowledge, sir.'

'Well, you would, wouldn't you? You're a policeman.' Conway, vindicated, was in glowingly benevolent mood. 'Get it off the premises, Alec. *Now.*'

'But, sir . . .'

There was no one to argue with. Conway had had his golden moment and relished it, and that was that.

After the chief inspector had left the locker room, Peters went down on his hands and knees to gather up the widely wandering cans of lager. He was hard at it when Tony Stamp put his head round the door and began to laugh. There was something very special in that laugh. Sergeant Peters looked up fiercely.

'Did you put this in here?'

'Not personally, no, sarge.'

'Then what the hell . . .'

'The lads were sure he'd turn you over in the end, so they fed him a bit. And that's satisfied his vanity, and he wouldn't really regard you as a villain, anyway.'

'You expect me to say thanks a million?'

'The important thing,' said Stamp, scratching the side of his nose, 'is that the rest is still safe.'

Peters brightened up. 'That's all right, then. Only where are you keeping it now?'

'Maybe you'd better not know, sarge.'

Peters shovelled the cans temporarily back into his locker and strolled off along the corridor. To his surprise he passed PC Edwards in civvies: surprise, because Taffy had taken a week of his leave and was not expected back until Monday morning.

June Ackland seemed equally surprised. 'Hullo, Taff. Been called in for emergency nights? Some flap we haven't been notified about yet?'

'No, just wondered if anyone fancied a drink, like.' As several of the others shuffled past in plain clothes, on their way home or to the pub, he looked quizzically at them and then back at June. 'I . . . well, I've just put Mary on the late train home, see. She's going house-hunting.'

June Ackland risked an uncertain, half-understanding or misunderstanding smile. 'Not a single-bed flat, I hope?'

His smile in return was rueful. 'No. A Welsh family retreat with room for a dog. And even kids.'

Full understanding dawned. She reached out and squeezed his arm. 'I think you're doing the right thing, Taff.'

'Yes,' he said despondently. Yes, I suppose so.'

Fifteen

'Writing a book?' said Taffy Edwards incredulously. 'She's being let out of here just like that to – '

'They call it a sabbatical, Taff.' Cathy Marshall ran an experienced eye down the form he had just handed across to her.

'Just to write a book,' Edwards marvelled. 'Wish I'd thought of that one.'

'The sort of book you'd write, we'd have half of Sun Hill rushing round the local newsagents seizing copies for the porn squad.'

Taffy went off, avoiding the eye of George Garfield in the corridor outside. Garfield was young and still terribly eager, just as Taffy had once been, looking for the action and wanting to chuck himself into it. How long would it take for him to grow weary and cynical, getting lazy, skiving off to avoid the boredom and the dirt and the dirty looks of the Conways and Cryers and the rest of them?

In the canteen it was all treated more lightheartedly. Someone had written out, with a felt-tip pen, whose bright colour might have struck a chord in Chief Inspector Conway's memory, a large notice announcing a farewell party in the *Freemason's Arms* that afternoon. It incorporated a crudely drawn cartoon of a character in a policeman's helmet furiously digging a tunnel below a high wall, and invited one and all to the celebration of PC Edwards' return to the Land of his Fathers. 'And all the other sheep shaggers,' someone had added even more crudely underneath.

It was quite a day for Sun Hill: two members of the team leaving on the same day. Taffy suspected that the farewell to

Inspector Frazer would be somewhat more decorous than his own. He was not looking forward to it. He had told that counsellor that he had never been one for drinking and getting loudmouthed with the boys. There would be a lot of backslapping and lot of stupid jokes – he had already had his fill of those – and a boisterous pretence of envying him. Deep down they wouldn't really envy him. And then it would be over, and he wouldn't see them again.

He was still far from sure that he really wanted to go.

He went back to the desk, eking out the last hours of his last tour of duty here. There was no great rush. Members of the public seemed to be having a carefree morning, having lost no handbags and not been mugged in the alley behind the supermarket.

'Ah, there you are, Taff.' Ken Melvin emerged from the CAD room. Edwards flinched. There was something too puritanical about Melvin as if police work was a religion offering stern tasks which ought not to be ducked. He waited for a grave frown, rubbing it in that flitting back to Wales was an abnegation of holy responsibilities. In fact Melvin seemed to have something different on his mind. He sounded almost diffident. 'Something I wanted to ask you, just between ourselves, before you go.'

Maybe he was going to enquire solicitously into the state of Taffy's soul, and then offer some embarrassing parting advice.

'What it is, Ken?' Taffy asked warily.

'Short-sleeved shirts.'

Taffy sighed. He might have guessed. 'How many?'

'What's the going rate?'

'One-twenty.'

'Right, I'll have 'em both off you.'

Melvin moved away with unexpected speed. He had become aware of the approach of Sergeant Cryer.

The sergeant leaned on the counter. For once he appeared to be at a loss for words. Taffy could do nothing to help. It was yet another of the awkward moments in this in-between morning.

'Quiet so far?' Cryer managed at last.

'Deadly.'

'Good. If by some unfortunate circumstance we do get any punters while you're here, for pity's sake don't upset them, offend them, or abuse them. Under no circumstances lay hands on them, and run like hell if they try to hit you.'

Edwards forced a smile. 'I'm not going to screw up my transfer by getting into trouble on my last day.'

'No, I suppose I can trust you on that score.' Cryer was suddenly harsh. 'You've done your best to stay out of harm's way all the time you've been here.' Before Edwards could protest, he went on brusquely: 'Now, the business about the final forms . . .'

'Yes, skipper, the forms. I've already done the one for Cathy – '

'I'm talking about the ones from Area. There's been a bit of a Horlicks up there – '

'With all due respect,' said Edwards grimly, 'it won't be the first bureaucratic booby-trap in the story of my transfer, will it?'

Cryer flared up. 'Don't give me any old buck, Edwards. This is going to get done and it's going to get done *right* if that's the only thing in your Metropolitan career that *is* done right.'

'If you say so, sarge.'

It would be nice to be transported in the twinkling of an eye to the top of a Welsh mountain, and get shot of all this. Right up to the last second they were going to harass him, the way they had always done.

Cryer said: 'It's difficult making it look all neat and happy all round, because they've spent tens of thousands of pounds trying to make you into a police officer, and they don't see why the sheep should have the benefit. But that's all blood under the bridge. This is a genuine cock-up with the forms. You should have been to Area, but they don't want you trailing round there on your uniform day, so they've sent the

167

forms here. You'll get them from Mr Conway, after you've had your chat with Mr Brownlow at 1.30.'

'Right, sarge.' Edwards stared into the distance.

'And before you fill them in, you'll see me. Understood? I don't want a lot of old rubbish going down in all that space provided. We don't want any works of fiction going out of these premises.'

'Sarge?'

'Yes?'

'On the subject of writing, like, what's all this stuff that Inspector Frazer's going to be doing?'

'Whatever it is, you're not likely to get an autographed copy.'

Detective Inspector Frank Burnside stood in the doorway of her office and said: 'Putting me in your memoirs, Chrissie?'

Inspector Frazer stacked copies of the *Police Review* on the desk beside an equally tall, teetering pile of books which she had been fishing out of her desk draweres. She shredded a few pieces of paper into the waste basket, and nudged her correspondence tray to make sure nothing had been trapped beneath it.

'I'm not writing a book, Frank,' she said. 'It's a thesis.'

'All right, a book with no pictures.' Burnside picked up Reiner's study of politics and the police, glanced inside, and shut it rapidly. 'And what's it all in aid of?'

'The topic,' said Frazer patiently, 'is a Comparative Study of Women's Career Patterns in the Police Force and in Private Industry and Commerce.'

'You won't half get bored. I got bored while you were telling me the title.'

'As a matter of fact I'm looking forward to spending some time in an academic environment, with people who can offer me some intellectual stimulation.'

'You'll miss the adrenalin.'

'There's a lot of things I won't miss, Frank, I can tell you that.'

'It didn't have to be like this, Chrissie.'

There was a sudden twist of what seemed genuine pain in his voice. It was not easy for Frank Burnside to give himself away like that. Pausing with a sheaf of papers in her hand, she looked at him across the accumulation of books and documents which represented a sizable part of her life and work here.

'What's that supposed to mean?'

'I've told you before. That liaison scheme we drew up, the way we were close to getting Brownlow to see it. We could have been a *team* here – CID and uniformed branch together instead of shooting off in every direction. Together we could run rings round the pillocks in this nick.' He took a deep breath, and tried to reassert his usual brash manner. 'Mind you, I can do that on my own, but I wish I'd had you along – for the ride.'

She could see that it was well meant. Perhaps if it had been talked through a year or so ago . . . No: she would not let her thoughts waver. He really had not grasped the first principle, so far as she was concerned. She said: 'Can't you see I'm only interested in making it in my own terms, in my own right?'

'The point is,' he said heavily, 'if you were making it, you wouldn't be bottling out to your ivory tower, to write the umpteen-millionth bellyache about women's troubles. Remember what I told you after that appraisal of yours?' He hesitated in the doorway, then saw that there would be no answer, and went out.

When the door had closed behind him, Christine Frazer leaned against the desk. She remembered all too well. That was the trouble: remembering the accumulated bitternesses, and the chances thrown away because nobody would listen, she knew it was time to get out of this oppressive atmosphere. Yet she hated to go, defeated. Hated the thought of Conway congratulating himself on having been right about her.

There had been an unfavourable report on her behaviour during the assault course. Hers was not the only one. The men in charge there had been particularly anxious to sneer at

169

the women and suggest they should stick to office jobs. At Sun Hill she had been expected to take sexist jokes and not throw them back in the grinning faces. 'One of the boys' was what you had to be. She had seen it in the way that the WPCs had been treated, which had made her tougher on them than she would otherwise have been, just to prove to them that they were as good as the rest. You tried to grow a hard skin. And still they either made more concessions than you had ever demanded; or without warning they turned on you. Not that Chief Inspector Conway could ever have been accused of inconsistency. From the start he had regarded her as an intruder and made things awkward every inch of the way. Then there was the ultimate insult of his damning official appraisal. She knew that even Chief Superintendent Brownlow had been taken aback, and had tried to find ways of sorting things out without too much unpleasantness. Brownlow was a great one for dodging unpleasantness. But this time it had not worked.

Frazer banged her desk in a sudden fury. All she achieved was the dislodgement of a pile of books on to the floor. The breeze of her departure from the office caused a further descent to the floor, this time of the cards bearing farewell messages of goodwill which had been propped on the skimpy mantelpiece over the long-redundant gas fire.

She passed PC Edwards in the corridor, and instinctively said: 'Oh, Edwards, I thought you'd gone.'

He looked at her in what might have been shared sympathy. 'Not yet, ma'am. Not quite yet.'

She was tempted to ask him to join the little group of well-wishers to which she had been invited in the Chief Super's office. The thought of the faces of the rest of them would have been almost worth it. But it would not have been fair on Edwards. The two of them smiled in nervous non-communication, and passed by.

After dumping some documents on Cathy Marshall she returned to her office, to find that someone had hastily scooped up the cards and set them in a mish-mash back on the ledge. There was a large new card in the very centre of the desk. It was from Chief Superintendent Brownlow. From a distance it looked very glossy and impressive. The picture was that of a shining horse, head proudly raised, against a background of undulating meadows. Frazer was quite touched. It implied a certain acknowledgement of style, breeding, quality.

She turned the card over. On the back was a printed note about the painter and his subject. She might have expected a prize-winning stallion or, if Brownlow had had a sense of humour, a troublesome mare. It depended on what he truly, genuinely thought of her. From the details, she doubted if he had given it any thought whatsoever: the painting was that of a gelding. So much for official appraisals!

PC Edwards left his post in front office and made his way reluctantly towards the stairs.

Reg Hollis appeared with uncharacteristic bonhomie. 'Here, Taffy, me old china plate.'

'I'm off to see Brownlow right now, Reg.'

'Won't take a minute.'

'Look, if it's about the kitty for the bar, I know some of the lads have put in more for their leaving do's, but some of them have been a lot better placed financially . . .'

'Not about that at all, old son.' Hollis put an arm round Edwards' shoulders. 'I want to talk to you – between ourselves, right? – about long-sleeved shirts. How are you placed?'

Edwards shook him off and went up the stairs to Chief Superintendent Brownlow's office. It was just another grisly episode in a grisly programme. Not one word of it could possibly mean anything any more.

He tapped on the door. A muffled voice answered. He assumed that this was an invitation to come in; but found that the reason for the muffled quality was that Brownlow had a mouthful of peanuts and was grunting over the lid of a case of wine which refused to be freed from its staples.

171

'Oh, um . . . um . . . yes, Edwards. Come in.' Brownlow swallowed, choked on a few fragments, and waved towards the chair facing his desk.

Edwards sat down. Brownlow edged round the desk and fumbled through his papers to find the brief memo listing all the things he ought to know about the PC's history at Sun Hill. Edwards offered no helpful nudge.

'Just gearing up,' Brownlow filled in time with a wave of the hand at the little bowls of nuts and biscuits and the cases of wine, 'for Inspector Frazer's leaving party.'

'I realised that,' said Edwards levelly.

'Of course, you'll be raising hell with the lads over at the . . . um . . . the *King's Head*, right?'

'The *Freemason's Arms*.'

'I know it well.' Brownlow extracted a sheet from the pile and looked relieved. 'Well, Edwards.' He settled back in his chair. 'Or Taffy, as you prefer to be called.'

'As a matter of fact, sir – '

'Yes, Taffy?'

'As a matter of fact I prefer being called Francis. But nobody's bothered with that so far. I get called Taffy here because of being Welsh. Bit ironical, really, spending a lot of time at Hendon being taught not to treat people as stereotypes, and then I found out I was one. A minor point, of course.'

'Mm.' Brownlow fiddled with the memo, and cast a none too surreptitious glance at his watch. 'Well, ah, Francis, I'd like us to continue this informal chinwag, but duty calls for both of us, as ever.' He pretended not to notice Edwards' meaning glance at the wine and nibbles, and got up, holding out his hand. 'It merely remains for me to express our heartfelt thanks for your contribution to our work here at Sun Hill. I know that your training and experience as a Metropolitan Police Officer will stand you in good stead in Cardiff.'

Cardiff? Edwards, shaking hands, wondered where this possibility had floated up from. 'Actually I'm not going – '

'And I want to wish you and . . . er . . .' Brownlow sought for a Christian name which he had never bothered to check on before, and looked helpless. Edwards left him that way. 'Want to wish you and Mrs Edwards every happiness in your new life.'

Edwards freed his hand. 'Thank you, Mr Brownlow.'

Brownlow ventured a quick glance at the memo on his desk, and tried to read it at an angle. 'Oh, and thank you for your dedicated and sportsmanlike captaincy of the badminton team, even though we didn't bring home any trophies this year.'

As Welshmen go, Taffy Edwards was unusual in many ways, not least of them being a complete lack of interest not merely in rugger but in any form of sporting exercise. As for *badminton* . . . More and more he felt himself trapped in a surreal, impossible world. Nowhere else could be as crazy as this. He was glad to make his escape, even though his next port of call was Chief Inspector Conway's office.

Conway's greeting was as tart as he might have expected, though not quite in the form he had expected.

'Oh. I thought you'd already gone.'

'I was told there were some forms, sir.'

Conway drew a sheaf of papers from his tray. 'Here we are. Now, these have to be filled in by you, and you'll have to do it here at the station today because we don't want you trailing over to Area – '

'Sergeant Cryer explained.'

'Good.' Conway was obviously impatient to rattle it all off and get away somewhere in a hurry: probably to the free drinks in Brownlow's office. 'Now, these forms are useful to the police in formulating and monitoring their policies and procedures, particularly as regards personnel.' He looked down the top sheet. 'You're being asked your reasons for leaving the Metropolitan Police – '

'I've already said all that.'

'Don't interrupt me when I'm telling you something. You have to put it all on these forms.'

Conway continued a recitation which began slowly to give

173

Edwards a tremor of pleasure. He was being asked to say if he had been in any way dissatisfied with the service. He should record any suggestions he had for improvements. Conway looked up warily but said that he should be quite frank with any criticisms of senior management, along with any comments on such matters as manpower levels and morale in the service. The whole point of the exercise like this would of course be lost if his response was not full and perfectly frank.

Edwards kept a straight face with difficulty. Perhaps this was just one bit of today's routine which could prove pleasurable. Inspector Frazer was not the only person who could write a thesis. The sooner he could dash it off – full and perfectly frank, according to instructions – the sooner he could get across to the *Freemason's Arms*, in a better mood than he had anticipated.

Conway was shaking his hand and then passing the forms across to him. 'Just one thing. You're to speak to Sergeant Cryer before you fill the forms in.'

Edwards hurried downstairs and found Bob Cryer waiting for him, already opening the door into the comparative tranquillity of one of the interview rooms.

'Should be all right in here for a bit.'

Edwards was now anxious to press on without interruption. 'I'm supposed to see the Stores Liaison Officer, and then get across the road – guest of honour, sort of.'

Cryer said bleakly: 'I want to make sure these forms are done right.'

'Mr Conway briefed me. I've got to put down all my criticisms and complaints. He said I've got to be full and frank or there's no point.'

Cryer gave him a long, hard stare. 'Well, what *I've* got to say is what the Sergeant Personnel would have to say if you were doing this at Area Office. He'd say *don't* criticise.'

'But the whole point – '

'I'm telling you something. He'd say don't burn any bridges. You never know in this life. Wales might not suit you

174

after all. The sheep might bite you. The Sons of Glyndwr might decide you're a traitor and set fire to your house.'

'I know what I'm doing.'

'However you feel now, you might want to come back. You slag off the Metropolitan Police in writing, and you'll never darken our door again. That's a promise.'

Cryer touched the edge of the table. Edwards put the forms on it, sat down, and took out his pen. 'I might just as well sign my name with an X and go off across the road for a couple of pints.'

'It's up to you. Everything's up to you now.' Cryer glanced towards the door. 'Looks like a clearance sale round here. I've got to look in at Frazer's knees-up. But there's one more thing I'd like to say now.' The edge of his voice was jagged, awkward. 'We've had our ups and downs, Taff. I've spoken a bit sharpish to you on more than one occasion.'

Now it was getting embarrassing. 'All part of the job, I suppose,' mumbled Edwards.

'But it's been intended for your own good, and the good of the job.' Cryer held out his hand. 'So if the air's cleared between us, I want to wish you the very best of luck in Wales.'

'Thanks, sarge.'

'Oh. One other little thing.'

'Sarge?'

'You got any lined gloves?' asked Cryer hopefully.

Sixteen

A trestle table had been carried into Chief Superintendent Brownlow's office, and alongside the little saucers of cheese biscuits and stuffed olives were a few plates of sandwiches and canapés with clingfilm. Most of the party in the room, waiting for the arrival of the guest of honour and a formal invitation to eat, were filling in time with the peanuts and dishes of savoury crisps on a filing cabinet. Sergeant Alec Peters, scorning such diffidence, lifted a corner of clingfilm and extracted a shrimp sandwich. After brief contemplation he was further tempted by half a gherkin embedded in cheese on a small cracker.

Brownlow stood at the door, welcoming newcomers with a large smile and a pat on the arm.

'Come on in, Frank, join the party.'

Detective Inspector Burnside looked round the collection of decorous figures, making stilted conversation in an effort to avoid talking shop; and failing.

'No danger of this getting out of hand, is there?' he asked.

Brownlow managed an indulgent chuckle. 'Get yourself a glass of Chablis, Frank.'

Burnside looked gloomily at the sparse array of bottles and rather small glasses. As a probationer handed him a none too generous measure in a glass, he heard Conway behind him muttering to Brownlow.

'As I was saying, there've been these ridiculous rumours. And you know we've had a lot of attitude from her about this whole business. She may be harbouring a grudge.'

'Christine? Well, you're the one who's had a down on her, Derek. I'm sure she knows I've always played fair by her.'

Burnside grinned to himself at this smooth demonstration of Brownlow washing his hands. Then he tasted the wine, and stopped grinning.

'Tom!' Brownlow was in booming mood again. 'Welcome. I know you're something of a connoisseur, Tom. Let me know what you think of the Chablis.'

'From your usual source, sir?'

'It is indeed.'

'Oh.' Sergeant Penny moved glumly towards the drinks table.

Bob Cryer was hard on his heels. 'Sorry to be late, sir. Just been putting Edwards straight.'

'Edwards?' The Chief Super rummaged through his memory. 'Ah, yes. Sad loss for the badminton team.' Leaving Cryer baffled, he boomed even louder. 'Christine! The guest of honour!'

It was the official signal for everyone to relax. The clingfilm came off the plates, the guests formed into little knots, juggling acts were done with glasses and small plates, and each group shuffled at intervals around Christine Frazer, making the obvious jokes about leaving the comforts of Sun Hill in order to sell her steamy memoirs to the News of the Screws. She had heard most of it before, over these last few weeks, and had all the stock answers off pat. But she tackled it with aplomb, smiled, and agreed or joshed her questioner, and circulated amiably.

Conway watched with some apprehension. 'I hope she's not getting drunk.'

'Don't worry, Derek. In my speech I'll try to defuse any tensions by the injection of a little humour.'

Conway flinched. For some reason this promise failed to reassure him. In spite of his doubts about drink he drifted off in search of one, trying to get close to the table dominated by three of the sergeants.

'I reckon they'll give us another woman,' Cryer was saying.

Peters, on his fourth sandwich, nodded sagely. 'Equal opportunities.'

'Probably be a one-legged, black, lesbian single parent, then,' Tom Penny offered.

Brownlow moved possessively closer to Christine Frazer, asserting his control of the proceedings but ensuring that his whole manner was a decorous one, in no danger of being misinterpreted or used against him in her thesis.

'So you'll soon be at it, Christine.'

'Sir?'

'Nose to the grindstone, scribbling away.'

'Thinking a lot before I do the actual writing.'

'Of course, of course. Er . . . mainly a sociological approach, your thesis, I suppose? General rather than . . . er . . . specific?'

'With a strong input of organisational theory and social psychology, of course.'

'Of course.' Brownlow thought for a moment, then said: 'My nephew's doing a thesis at Manchester.'

'Really?'

'Polymer sciences.' He dug into the recesses of his mind for a few useful shreds. 'Long chain molecules.'

Two of the relief sergeants in the far corner of his office were laughing too loudly about something on the window-sill. Peters seemed to be eating too fast, and Burnside was winking at Christine Frazer and trying to beckon her over. It was, Brownlow judged, time for the formalities.

It took him a couple of minutes to find the notes he had made earlier today. Then, having said 'Ladies and gentlemen,' and then archly 'Lady and gentlemen', and waited for the slurping and shuffling to stop, he launched into his speech. It took him a few stumbling sentences to get into his stride, as he discovered that he had forgotten the joke he had meant to start with, but after a while he began to like the whole sound of it. It might even give the departing Frazer a few ideas for her own work. If she asked him for a copy he could have it typed up and sent to her. Might get a mention in the grateful acknowledgements at the beginning of her completed text.

'The past few years have seen the rôle of the police in

contemporary society undergoing agonising reappraisal and rapid change. In this process we must all feel there have been losses as well as gains. But one of the clear gains has been the increasing appreciation of the contribution of women to police work. Not so long ago, when it was put to a very distinguished police officer that the number of WPCs should be increased, he replied in light-hearted vein . . .' Brownlow held his notes closer to his eyes and recited the wording carefully. '"Is recruiting so bad that we now have to breed our own, as we attempted to do with dogs and horses?"' He chortled, and looked round.

There was a deathly hush. Conway looked at the tips of his boots. Burnside looked at his watch. Frazer looked incredulous and then contemplative, as if storing up a bit of evidence to add to her thesis.

Disconcerted, Brownlow stumbled on. 'Er . . . a whimsical notion entirely dispelled by the sterling service women officers have given in every field of policing. Their commitment and enthusiasm are typified in our colleague – and *friend*,' he added hopefully, 'Christine Frazer.'

There was a smattering of applause, and some polite nods in Frazer's direction. When Brownlow had trailed off to a finish, it was her turn. The sergeants applauded vigorously. A relief inspector, whose presence here had not been explicitly accounted for to any of the Sun Hill regulars, made a slow and mildly disconcerting inspection of each face, as if making mental notes for some future personal assessment. Conway risked a glance at Brownlow, who carefully did not respond. Of course it was a routine business, it would soon be over, Frazer wouldn't say anything disparaging, not on a jolly occasion like this. Of course she wouldn't.

Christine Frazer edged towards the centre of the room.

'Someone once said to me that leaving parties were very curious occasions. Your senior officers say such kind and encouraging things about you.' She paused, turning her wide-eyed gaze upon one face after another. 'If they'd only said them earlier, you wouldn't have wanted to leave.' There was a fraught silence. Conway gulped. After leaving them all to stew for a few interminable seconds, Frazer went on: 'But that's a terribly cynical view, and one that I certainly couldn't support from my experience at Sun Hill. Since I came here I've been frequently touched . . .' Frank Burnside smirked into his empty glass. 'Touched,' she said, 'by the support and co-operation I've received from senior officers and colleagues at all levels. It has been an education for me, in more ways than one, and I'm deeply grateful. It would be wrong to single out individuals for thanks, but special mention must be made of our Chief Superintendent, Mr Brownlow, a never-failing source of advice and encouragement.'

This time Brownlow was prepared to exchange a glance with Conway. So she wasn't going to flip her lid: she wasn't burning any bridges.

Bonhomie burned bright again. The bottles were emptied, a few crumbs were left on the plates, and everyone was shaking hands, and Cryer was chatting respectfully to the watchful relief inspector. When he moved away, Peters said: 'Seem to be making a hit with that character – Monroe, isn't it?'

'Glad you've got the name right. And you'd better try and make a hit, too. That's likely to be our new guv'nor.'

'Strewth! We didn't know when we were well off. At least Frazer had legs.'

Frazer was making a brief farewell circuit, finishing up at the door with Brownlow and Conway. Conway's grip was the firmest and most sincere of the lot. He wanted an upstanding, irreproachable mention in her thesis. She smiled tolerantly but unpromisingly, and walked along the corridor to the top of the stairs with Frank Burnside.

'Listen, we'll have to get together,' he suggested.

'I'll try to let you know when I'm settled.'

It was unconvincing enough for him to grimace and head off towards the CID office.

At the foot of the stairs she found PC Edwards, clutching a holdall and looking as if the whole building had suddenly become strange to him, so that he could not decide which direction to take.

'Hello, Taff. I thought you'd gone.'

'Not quite, ma'am.'

'Been keeping out of trouble on your last day?'

'Well.' He smiled a deep, strange smile, as if recording some inner satisfaction. 'Well, that remains to be seen. And you?'

'Yes,' she said, a trifle wistfully. 'I've been very well behaved.'

There was really nothing else to say. They hesitated for a moment. 'Er, will you be coming over the road,' Edwards ventured, 'for a drink?'

'I'll try to look in. But there's still a lot to sort out.'

'Yes. Well, all the best, then.'

They shook hands awkwardly, and she left him standing there, still apparently uncertain; though surely the whole gang were waiting for him in the pub, and that was the obvious place to make for?

Reg Hollis had decided to take charge of the entire proceedings, and the rest of them had let him do so. It was not that they particularly trusted or respected him; but since he was a fusspot by nature, it was easier to leave him to it than to try doing things piecemeal, with Reg always interfering and getting tripped over.

In the function room of the *Freemason's Arms* he took a managerial look around, and began moving things. Chairs and tables which did not suit his taste were nudged to one side of the room, then back into the middle. The microphone on the low stage did not please him. He tapped it three times, whistled into it, snapped 'Testing, testing, one-two-three', and then glared across at the barmaid glumly polishing glasses. 'Hey, Tina. It's not working.'

'Well, it ain't plugged in, is it?'

'Oh.' He didn't like her attitude, or her clothes. Her sloppy sweatshirt had seen better days, and the tracksuit bottoms did not match, even according to the standards of the corner boutique – or junkshop. 'I see you haven't bothered with a cocktail frock.'

'Not after last time.'

'It won't be like that.'

They heard a burst of raucous laughter, and the bang of an outer door. Hollis recognised the voices of Stamp and Quinnan, obviously warming up with low jokes before they had even reached the bar. Tina might not have identified the actual voices, but she recognised the tone and its implications.

'I don't see anything funny about ice cubes,' she said. 'Not down your cleavage, when you're trying to do a job.'

'It's not going to be like that today,' Hollis assured her. 'It's a friendly do for an old mate, just saying goodbye and wishing him all the best, that's all.'

The door burst open to admit the first two arrivals. Stamp looked round the room and demanded: 'Where is he, then?'

'Still getting sorted out, I suppose,' said Hollis.

'Has he handed over the dosh?'

Hollis nodded towards Tina. 'Behind the bar.'

'That's all right, then.' Stamp headed towards her. 'I'll have a pint of lager.'

'Make that two, darling,' said Quinnan.

She began to pull the first pint, watching the two of them suspiciously.

Hollis said with an assumption of austere control: 'I was explaining to the young lady that this is a respectable occasion, and there'll be no sort of – '

'You want to watch him.' Stamp leaned across the bar, leering. 'He's well known.'

'On no account agree to handle his helmet,' Quinnan sniggered.

Hollis perservered. 'I was explaining that this do is not going to get out of order, because our guest of honour is not a wild man or a maniac.'

'You can say that again.'

'He's a short streak of Welsh misery, as a matter of fact,'

182

said Stamp. He reached for his pint. 'But I'll have a drink off him.'

As the two of them turned away from the bar, Hollis sidled closer. 'One thing I've fixed, anyway,' he boasted. 'Got a bird lined up. Comes in, takes her clothes off . . . only tastefully, of course . . .'

'Of course.' Quinnan wiped froth from his lips. 'Has to be tasteful, that sort of thing.'

'Then she makes him dance about with his hands on her bristols.'

'Singing "There'll be a welcome on the hillsides" while he's at it?'

'Frazer would just love that notion,' observed Stamp. 'Sexual harassment – isn't that what she's writing about in this best-seller of hers?'

'Only in the Force. Not off-duty. It's all right then.'

Tina inspected the drip tray behind the bar as if consulting an oracle and coming to the conclusion that her worst fears would soon be realised.

The room began to fill up. All at once there was a queue along the bar, clamouring for drink and getting impatient as Tina tried to cope with a recalcitrant tap. A young man hired by Hollis to provide the music added to the din by turning knobs and producing screeching noises from the speakers. Too late Hollis realised that in his anxiety to supervise everything he had omitted to grab himself a drink at the start. Now there was no way through. He tried to assert himself. 'Miss . . . *miss* . . . Tina . . . Look, you lot, I've been getting everything lined up and it's time I . . .'

'Come on, chief redcoat.' Stamp had somehow managed to get himself another pint. 'When we going to have some music?'

'Well, we haven't officially started the proceedings yet. I mean, until Taff gets here – '

'Oh, stuff him. Let's have some sounds.'

'If I could just get myself a drink first – '

'We can't wait that long. Come on, make with the music.'

Resignedly Hollis turned towards the DJ on the platform. The speakers began belching something not very different from the original screeches, but this time supported by a steady beat.

Each time the door opened, heads turned to see if Edwards was at last putting in an appearance. Almost everybody else came in. Ted Roach made for the bar and commandeered a stool. Tosh Lines edged towards the far end, thankfully grabbed a pint, and hoped that the free booze would last the evening: he was only here because he had promised his wife he wouldn't need to put his hand in his pocket all evening. Jimmy Carver looked round repeatedly for Edwards: it seemed a long time since they had joined Sun Hill within a few weeks of each other, and the place would be strange without him. Still there was no sign. Sergeant Cryer keeping him in after school for not having done his homework?

Viv Martella and Norika Datta got their drinks and leaned with their backs against the wall as a precaution against Tony Stamp's habit of pinching bottoms. He looked around for another victim, but they lacked what he fancied. Considering a different approach, he sidled up to Martella, who wedged herself even more firmly against the wall.

'Viv, I've been wanting to have a serious talk with you.'

'I've had my official appraisal, thanks. From Inspector Frazer, and look what happened to *her*. Not much you can contribute at this stage.'

'No, seriously. I mean, I've always admired you. The poise, the . . . the . . .'

'This is the lager talking.'

'No, straight up. You're an independent woman in your own right.' It was no use. He could not resist it: 'And dead horny.'

She smiled witheringly. 'That sounds more like the real Stamp.'

'Come on, Viv, you're not a teaser, I know that. Let's be adult. How about it?'

184

'Let's be adult,' she agreed, 'and drop the subject, and stay on good terms.'

'But it'll only take a minute.'

Martella glared at him and pushed past, on her way to join Claire Brind.

The noise grew. Some men at the bar had virtually forgotten the reason for being here. There was free booze, so why ask questions? Turnham was trying to chat up the barmaid, which took some doing as she dashed to and fro trying to serve everybody at once. Ted Roach also concentrated on her at regular intervals, but only in order to have his whisky glass replenished.

Hollis began to fret. Where the hell was Taffy Edwards?

There was a sudden scream. Dave Quinnan had helped himself to a handful of cubes from the ice bucket on the counter, crept up on Tim Able, and tipped them down inside his collar.

'See?' The barmaid tucked the top of her sweatshirt closely under her chin. 'I knew it.'

Into the middle of all the men and women in their civvies came a uniformed WPC. The girls looked at her curiously. Nobody recognised her. She took a card from her top pocket and said: 'Is there a Mr Edwards here, please?'

'*Mister* Edwards?' said Ted Roach blearily. 'A bit premature, I'd have thought. This time next week, maybe, or maybe technically it's tomorrow, depending on . . .' He shrugged, gave up, and returned to the whisky.

The uniformed girl looked peevishly around. 'Well, if there ain't no Edwards I can't do nuffink.'

Light dawned on Claire Brind. She remembered her own performance at Yorkie Smith's farewell do, and liked to think she had looked a lot subtler and more stylish than this hired, bored stripper. The truth dawned on Hollis, too. He elbowed his way through the crowd, caught the girl's arm, and dragged her towards the stage.

'You Mr Edwards?'

'He hasn't shown up. If you wouldn't mind – '

'Look, I've got another booking half an hour from now. Can't hang about.'

'I'll stand in for him,' said Hollis wildly.

There was a chorus of hoots from the audience.

The girl said: 'Well, make yer minds up.'

'I'm his representative,' said Hollis.

Drearily the girl read from the card with which she had been provided. 'Well, Mr Edwards, your car is illegally parked, and I'm going to have to arrest you.'

Hollis grabbed the microphone. This was his moment of glory. 'It's a fair cop! Boom, boom!'

'It's very hot in here,' said the girl mechanically. 'I think I will take my clothes off.'

There was a quick release strap inside her uniform tunic which was decidedly not official issue. The whistles began as the tunic opened, and grew shriller as she reached behind her back to release another strap. She advanced on Hollis, who looked as if he was having half a dozen birthdays all at one go.

It was Hollis's treat, all right.

But where the hell was Edwards?

He had sat for a long, depressing time in that interview room with the official forms spread out on the table before him. The questions were so simple, and there was plenty of space to write the answers. He could see from the phrasing of the questions exactly what he was supposed to say; and knew from Sergeant Cryer exactly what he must not say. Fill in the obvious meaningless clichés and be done with it. He was leaving anyway. It made no difference one way or the other.

Yet something had gone on sizzling inside him. Say the obvious, expected thing, and then go and make the obvious, expected jokes and take the obvious, expected ribbing from the boys. Sink a few pints, and everyone would remember you as not a bad type, poor old Taffy, sorry to see him go, one of the characters, stupid Welsh git.

He had written a couple of lines in one of the spaces, all

nice and neat and inoffensive, according to the recipe. Then he had looked at them; looked at his watch and thought how easy it would be to scribble some hurried, equally predictable stuff in the other sections, and then go across the road and drown the memory of it.

Either that, or this was a last chance to show some guts. Which Sergeant Cryer had sometimes implied, and other times said outright, he hadn't got.

It had taken him fifteen minutes to scratch out the sensible lines which would have burned no bridges, and add the crazily truthful lines which might set every bridge along the Thames on fire if the fire brigade were not skilled at containing such blazes before they ever really took hold.

Good luck to the fire brigade, then!

When he had finished he went to the duty sergeant's office and laid the papers on the desk.

'Leave this for Sergeant Cryer?'

Sergeant Utley looked up. 'Edwards? I thought you'd gone.'

Taffy proceeded to the property store to hand over his uniform. The stores liaison officer dropped the items one by one unemotionally into a large brown paper bag as he checked off the printed list. In the end there remained only Edwards' helmet, stick and whistle.

'Right. So far you're missing two short-sleeved shirts, one long-sleeved shirt, and one pair of lined gloves.'

'That's right.'

The SLO winked. 'Saved your mates a few quid, then. They couldn't replace those bits for the price we're going to have to charge you.'

Edwards pushed his helmet across the counter.

Again the SLO looked knowing and sympathetic. 'Er . . . you sure? I mean, in my experience lads invariably lose their helmet, stick and whistle.'

'Well, I haven't.'

'Souvenirs,' the SLO prompted. 'If you know what I mean.'

187

'I'm transferring, aren't I? I'll get new ones.'

'Even so, as mementoes of your . . . well, you know . . . *Metropolitan* police service . . .'

Taffy Edwards looked at the remaining items. Very carefully he picked up the stick and whistle, dropped them into the upturned helmet, and handed over the lot. The SLO calculated the space left in his paper bag and looked at Edwards with no remaining sympathy. By refusing to take his trophies, Edwards had clearly insulted the flag.

On his way out, in civvies and with his holdall, he passed Sergeant Utley, who said: 'Oh, still here?' And it was as he paused at the foot of the stairs that Inspector Frazer said it: 'I thought you'd gone, Taffy.'

Impulsively he had asked her over to the pub for a drink with the rest of them. When at last he summoned up the courage to push the door open and go out into the world, without looking back at the station, he wasn't sure whether she would come or even whether he would be there to greet her.

The noise from the *Freemason's Arms* was audible halfway down the street. He knew how it would swell as he opened the door and went in. They were well away already.

He stopped on the corner and now forced himself to look back at Sun Hill.

It was no good. He couldn't just walk into that pub as though it was a great occasion for a celebration. He managed, step by step, to cross the road and walk right past the main door. The noise poured out over him. There were shrieks, and a girl was shouting something, and then at the side entrance round the corner he saw Inspector Frazer and June Ackland, hesitating. He ought to go down and put on a big flourish, taking their arms and escorting them inside.

A girl with a coat wrapped round her shoulders came out and teetered towards a car waiting by the far pavement. She stopped for a moment, looked Frazer up and down with professional disdain, and giggled.

188

'Stone me, not another double booking! I just done the gig, love. You want to get on to the agency about this.'

Taffy Edwards looked away down the long, bleak street, and walked away into the bleak afternoon and whatever lay beyond. This time he did not look back.

Also by John Burke available from Mandarin Paperbacks

THE BILL 2

There is tension at Sun Hill Police Station, and
not just between the police and the villains.
Detective Inspector Galloway's marriage is on the
rocks, Sergeant Cryer is trying to hold his team
together and the word from on high is to cut costs
but not to drop standards.

But outside, on the streets of the East End, crimes
are being committed, and whether it is staking
out bank robberies, searching for missing school
girls, clearing up after a multiple collision or
arresting obstructive animal liberationists, the
private preoccupations of the force at Sun Hill
have to take second place to the strange and often
grim business of policing their patch.

THE BILL 3

Change is afoot at Sun Hill Police Station.
Detective Inspector Galloway's replacement is
soon to be revealed, meanwhile the nick is still
reeling from the announcement that the new
uniformed inspector is to be a woman.

New guvnors will bring with them new ways and
different working methods, but out in the manor,
the steady flow of crime does not pause for a
second. Whether it is abandoned babies, football
hooligans, stolen gardens or kidnapped
policemen, the coppers at Sun Hill – men and
women, uniformed and CID – must combat them
all, cope with the changes within their own
organization and still try to come up smiling . . .

A Selected List of Fiction Available from Mandarin

While every effort is made to keep prices low, it is sometimes necessary to increase prices at short notice. Mandarin Paperbacks reserves the right to show new retail prices on covers which may differ from those previously advertised in the text or elsewhere.

The prices shown below were correct at the time of going to press.

☐	7493 0003 5	**Mirage**	James Follett	£3.99
☐	7493 0134 1	**To Kill a Mockingbird**	Harper Lee	£2.99
☐	7493 0076 0	**The Crystal Contract**	Julian Rathbone	£3.99
☐	7493 0145 7	**Talking Oscars**	Simon Williams	£3.50
☐	7493 0118 X	**The Wire**	Nik Gowing	£3.99
☐	7493 0121 X	**Under Cover of Daylight**	James Hall	£3.50
☐	7493 0020 5	**Pratt of the Argus**	David Nobbs	£3.99
☐	7493 0097 3	**Second from Last in the Sack Race**	David Nobbs	£3.50

All these books are available at your bookshop or newsagent, or can be ordered direct from the publisher. Just tick the titles you want and fill in the form below.

Mandarin Paperbacks, Cash Sales Department, PO Box 11, Falmouth, Cornwall TR10 9EN.

Please send cheque or postal order, no currency, for purchase price quoted and allow the following for postage and packing:

UK   80p for the first book, 20p for each additional book ordered to a maximum charge of £2.00.

BFPO   80p for the first book, 20p for each additional book.

Overseas   £1.50 for the first book, £1.00 for the second and 30p for each additional book
including Eire thereafter.

NAME (Block letters) ....

ADDRESS ....

....

....